STORY MIX

Leonard Dawson

CONTENTS

Acknowledgments

An earlier version of A Photographic Memory was published on the website, Short-Story.me, in December of 2013.

An earlier version of Cemetery Dead Ahead was published on the website, Darker Times, in January of 2013, and was included in their Darker Times anthology, volume two.

Dead Lucky was published on the website, Short-Story.me, in May of 2010.

An earlier version of On the Take was published under the name Everyone's On the Take by Gypsy Shadow publishing in 2010.

Killer Lesson was published on the website, Darker Times, in January of 2013, and was included in their Darker Times anthology, volume two.

An earlier version of When Good Food Goes Bad was published as Food for Thought on the website, Perihelion Sci-Fi, in February 2013.

An earlier version of Z Haulers was published in June of 2017 by Hellfire Crossroads, and was included in their Hellfire Crossroads anthology, volume six, Horror with a Heart.

An earlier version of Zombies Are No Laughing Matter was published by Bride of Chaos in January of 2017, and was included in their 9 Tales Told in the Dark anthology, volume 21.

CEMETERY DEAD AHEAD

Standing all by myself next to my uncle's open coffin, I almost screamed when that one cloudy eye of his popped open and looked right at me as if he'd been lying in there playing dead, waiting for me to get close so he could frighten me.

All the kids called him "Old One-Eye" because he wore a patch over one eye, just like a pirate. And his good eye was so cloudy it was almost white. And they were all as scared of him as I was.

Then his thin white lips whispered, "Come here, Davy," and I ran away, pushing and shoving my way through the crowd at his wake, running as though my dead uncle had climbed out of that coffin to chase me. And when I got outside I ran some more, and I didn't stop running for a long, long time.

I guess folks were in a hurry to get rid of him because they put him in the ground later that same day. I probably should've told someone he wasn't really dead, but I didn't because I wanted him buried so he couldn't ever look at me with that scary eyeball again.

I didn't go to the burial service, and not just because the crazy old coot had scared me. I didn't want to miss out on

Trick or Treat. Yeah, that's right, my uncle died on Halloween. Halloween's no different than any other day when it comes to dying. So by the time they were putting sod over him a couple of hours later, the night was full of little ghouls and goblins collecting candy, the streetlights turning them into long, spider-thin, wildly-animated shadows slithering through the neighborhood.

The other kids shied away from me because mine was the scariest costume of all. One woman who opened the door to greet me even yelled to someone in the house, "Jesus, Harry, you gotta come see this kid's costume."

Another lady handing out candy just stood there with her mouth open after she saw me. When I reached into her bowl I said, "Boo," because I thought it'd be fun to make her scream. It wasn't. My ears rang from her shriek.

My bag was nearly full of candy when I spotted them half a block away, a gang of older boys standing around a little kid wearing a Superman costume, six of them, and all of them bigger and older than me. They looked kind of familiar, but then bullies all look alike, don't they?

One of them said something to the kid I couldn't hear. The little guy held his bag of candy behind his back then stuck his chin out defiantly and shook his head. Brave little guy; stupid too, and I already know what you're thinkin' - that I should've gone and helped him. Well, I've had my turn getting beat up. Now I'm smarter than that. And besides, how else is he gonna learn?

I watched them take the kid's bag of candy and push him to the ground, but I didn't stick around to see what they did to him next because one of them spotted me. He pointed at me and yelled, "Hey, look, it's that same kid from last year."

I turned around and ran away as fast as I could, as fast as I ran when my uncle scared me at the wake. And when I looked back over my shoulder they were coming after me. I can run really fast for my age, but those boys were bigger and their legs were longer.

I should've run to the nearest house where they were giving out candy, but I panicked, cutting across someone's lawn, running between two houses and through some shrubs. Then I rolled under an iron fence into the cemetery. I'd had the wild idea that I could hide there in the darkness, but as soon as I cleared that fence I felt the despair that sets in when you realize you've made a really bad decision you can't undo.

I headed for the mausoleums deep in the cemetery, beyond even the faintest glow of the streetlights. It would be dark there, as dark as any place on this earth ever gets, and the gravestones would be bigger, big enough to hide behind, if I could make it that far before those boys caught me.

I ran till my sides ached then stopped to catch my breath, leaning over to put my hands on my knees. Looking back, I saw six dark shapes backlit by far-off street lights spread out into a line that soon became an arc, the boys at the sides running the fastest, forming a semi-circle that would soon close around me. I couldn't outrun them but I ran anyway, trying to outrun the thought of what they'd do to me when they caught me, but how do you outrun what's in your head? And I knew they'd be extra mad when they caught me because I'd made them chase me. And there wasn't anyone around to stop them from beating me to a ragged, bloody pulp.

Why I thought of my bag of candy then I don't know, but I realized I didn't have it anymore and I couldn't remember when I'd dropped it. But I forgot all about my candy when those boys began to threaten me, yelling things like, "Hey, kid. You know what I'm gonna do to you? I'm gonna shove sticks in your eyes when I catch you," and, "We're gonna dig up a fresh grave and put you in with the stiff and cover you up with dirt."

I ran again, as fast as I could, swerving around the gravestones like a slalom skier. I caught glimpses of the shadowy figures running off to the sides, bullies closing the circle around me. In a few seconds I'd have to stop or I'd run right into them, and my back prickled with the expectation that at any moment hands would grab me from behind.

"There you are," someone yelled as I swerved around a large headstone, a blast of frosty air hitting me, as though the cry echoing off the gravestones around me had come to me on a North Wind. I slid to a stop on the grass, almost crashing into Old One-Eye and coming to a stop right in front of him.

I heard a collective gasp behind me. It was the bullies. They had me trapped, but I didn't dare take my eyes off the specter in front of me - Old One-Eye, wild-eyed and grinning like the crazy man people said he was.

I'd forgotten they'd buried him in that cemetery or I never would've cut through there. I wondered what a man who'd been buried alive would do to the kid who hadn't said anything, the kid who'd let them put him in the ground and cover him with dirt, but the crazy old coot seemed more interested in something behind me, so I spun around to see what he was looking at.

Turned out those tough kids weren't so tough after all. They were backing away from Old One-Eye. Then one of them broke and ran and they all scattered, the six of them running away in six different directions, running like the devil himself was after them. I saw a patch of moonlight twinkle in Old One-Eye's cloudy eyeball as he watched them run away.

Grinning like a lunatic, he yelled at them. "I'll show you what I do to bullies."

With the bullies gone and my uncle taking no notice of me, I decided to run for it, but as I spun around to make my escape a boney hand closed on my shoulder like a vise. Old One-Eye turned me around to face a headstone that read, "Here lies Davy Bryant, age ten, taken from his loving parents before his time."

When I saw my name etched in that stone I felt a chill inside that went all the way down to my bones. Sometimes we just know something even though all of our senses let us down, the way I knew it was me under that stone. I looked down at my body then and I could see right through to my bones, my flesh thin and wispy as though it was made of nothing thicker than dirty bath water.

Pieces of broken memories flashed before me then; me running from those same bullies last Halloween, and the one before that, and the one before that. Then I saw Old One-eye jump out at me from behind a tree. I saw myself run into the street, felt a car slam into me. The last thing I saw was me lying in the street with One-eye standing over me and my candy scattered all over the road and the other kids going after it like crows on road kill.

That's when the images stopped. I thought about the bullies and being dead, and was bewildered by it all, so I asked Old One-Eye, "If I'm dead, how come people can see me?"

He told me I'd drift among the living until I had accepted my death; and that I'd keep reliving that night until I did.

When I asked him why he was still around, he trained that cloudy eye of his on me and said, "Your mother sent me to find you that night. When I saw you running from those bullies I jumped out from behind a tree and yelled, "Boo," to scare them away. But I frightened you too. That's why you ran in front of the car that night, and you've been stuck here reliving the past until I make amends. That's what I tried to tell you when you were standing by my coffin at the funeral home. But now that I'm dead, we're going to teach those bullies a lesson they'll never forget."

Then I was glad to have Old One-eye on my side of forever.

EVANGELINE

When I saw Granny coming I yelled to Momma. "Hurry. Granny's coming and she's got a strange man with her."

I stood on the bare hardpan outside our front door waiting for Momma while I watched granny and the man coming down the hill, the two of them moving slow as molasses in the winter. Granny's really old and walking over the hill is terrible hard on her, so she never comes to our house unless it's something really important.

I know she's old because her body's all shriveled up like a dandelion after a dry spell, and because she always wears lots of clothes, even on the hottest days. And her face is as wrinkled as an old paper bag. She looked old when I was a little girl, and I'm all of eleven years old now

The man walking with her looked old too; not near as old as Granny but older than my daddy was when he left us. That was almost two years ago and there hasn't been a man around here since. And I couldn't ever remember seeing Granny with a man so I wondered who he was and why she brought him.

Momma asked, "Why all the fuss, Eve?" as she came outside and stood next to me. I like being called "Eve." I don't like being called "Evangeline," which is my real name, and what Granny calls me. Momma's name is Anne. She tells everybody she's thirty. Maybe she is. I can't tell. But she sure is pretty, even prettier 'n Granny's porcelain dolls.

Momma put a hand up to shade her face from the sun while she watched Granny and the strange man. Her plain white cotton dress, the one she made herself, fluttered in the hot dry wind, making noises like the curtains in the open window behind us.

It seemed like forever went by while we stood there watching them walk down the dirt path through the field grass. Granny stopped every once-in-a-while, stooping over and holding her hand on her chest. I think she was trying to catch her breath. Me, I can run all the way over the hill to Granny's big house.

We don't have a porch, and there's no shade to be had from the one half-dead tree in our yard, so there was no place for Granny to hide from the sun when she got here. Her face looked as white as the ash in our fireplace, and shiny, the way new skin looks when you peel off a scab. But Momma didn't invite her into the house and I know why – 'cause Granny would stay longer if she had a place to sit, and every time Granny comes here she starts in on Momma about driving Daddy away.

I figured the man Granny brought with her had to be a hobo because he had a knapsack slung over his shoulder, and because his old blue working man's clothes had almost no color left. His hat brim, which he had pulled down low, shaded his face from the sun and hid everything from me but his chin and beard stubble.

Standing there as tall and as skinny as my daddy, with his hands in his pockets, looking down like he was studying something in the dirt, reminded me of the time Daddy and I had to wait at the store for Momma while she picked out the cloth for her dress.

Struggling to talk between breaths, her skinny little arms shaking as though she had palsy, Granny lowered herself to rest on our bottom step, pleading with Momma in a voice that sounded as feeble as she looked. "Aren't you gonna give me something to drink?"

Momma told her to go get her own drink from the well.

After she said that it got quiet, except for Granny's breathing and the snapping sounds made by the wind blowing the curtains and momma's dress.

Drawing a long, raspy breath, Granny told Momma, "You got an ugly side to you. It's no wonder you couldn't keep a man around."

I think Granny liked to make my momma mad, and that's just what she did. I've seen Momma mad at me enough times to know she was real mad. "You referring to that good-for-nothing son of yours; the one that run off and left us here to starve while he lifted some other woman's skirts?"

Granny pointed a thumb back over her shoulder. "Maybe if you wasn't dried up like that hill yonder, my boy would've stayed."

Putting her arm around me and pulling me in tight to her side Momma told Granny, "Well thank God he wasn't around long enough to plant another seed in me. I got all I can do to feed this one."

Granny's throat must've been real dry because what she tried to say next came out sounding like someone walking on dead grass. She swallowed hard and started again. "Way I see it, it was your sinful ways drove him out."

I'd heard them arguing like that a thousand times and I didn't want to hear it all again, and I guess Momma didn't either because she told Granny, "Say what you came to say, then leave."

Granny twisted around sideways on the step to face us. "When I was at the feed store, I heard the fellers there talking about some evil men going around these parts raping and thieving and killin' and such."

Momma told her she was foolish, and that, "Those old men at the store like to talk. Seems like that's all they do. And I ain't got time for their foolishness, nor yours neither."

Granny shook her head at that. "You think you know everything, but Mrs. Warren at the Post Office told me she heard about 'em from the sheriff."

I guess Momma had had enough 'cause she told Granny,

"They won't come here. Hell, the road don't even come here. It stops on the other side of the hill. But you didn't come here to tell me about them men. You came here to spy on me, and see if maybe your son came back. Well you can see for yourself he ain't here."

Then Momma nodded her head at the man standing quietly in the baking-hot sun. "Who's he and what's he doing here?"

Granny squinted at Momma when she answered, like she didn't trust Momma. "I got work needs doin' at my place, so I went down to the shantytown near the rail yard and got me a hobo."

The man was quiet like Daddy, or maybe he was just scared of saying something with Momma and Granny acting mad. And he had big hands like my daddy. I wondered if he got them from working on machinery; seems like men who do that have big hands.

Sometimes when Daddy was still living here I snuck out to the hayloft and opened the trap door in the floor where Daddy dropped hay down for the cow. I sat and dangled my legs through the opening while I watched him working on farm machinery in the room down below.

I especially liked it when he worked until dark because then he'd hold my hand in his big strong hand when he walked me back to the house. And if I was a really good girl that day he'd tuck me into bed and I'd smell oil and old hay on him.

Momma asked Granny, "Why bring the hobo here?"

"I couldn't leave him at my house. He might've stole something."

"Ain't nothin here worth taking," Momma said, as she looked the man over.

"He's mine," Granny said. "I'm the one who went down there and got him."

Then shaking one of her bony little fingers at the man, she scolded him, even though he hadn't done a thing but stand there in the hot sun. "Maybe you like the look of her. Maybe you think something might come of it. Well, think about this: she's got no money to pay you but I do."

I had an idea what Granny meant by, "liking the look of her," and I wondered if he might get to like my momma, wondered what it'd be like if he stayed. And while I wondered that Momma asked the man his name.

He took his hat off, real courteous like, but held it up so it shaded his face from the sun. "You can call me Walker, ma'am."

"What's the rest of your name?"

"Walker's all the name I usually need, ma'am."

Granny shouted, "He's too old."

That made Momma mad again. "Look around you, old woman. There's a lot of work here needs doin', and if it don't get done soon, won't be nothin for us to eat come winter."

The man didn't look too old to me. I saw a little gray hair in the stubble on his chin, but his face wasn't droopy like Granny's. Hers looked like a beeswax candle that had been left out in the sun.

Then it was Momma's turn to scold the man. "I don't think Walker's your name, I think that's what you do. And I figure a man who'd hide his name from us is running from something. And whatever it is you're running from, I don't want it comin' 'round here looking for you."

The way he said, 'Ma'am," to her I couldn't tell if he was agreeing with her or not.

Then she asked him if he could do an honest day's work without dying in the heat, and I thought maybe I was wrong, maybe she did want him to stay.

He said, "Yes, ma'am," real casual like, but Momma looked at him the way she looks at me when she thinks I've told her a lie.

Momma gave me a nudge toward the stairs. "Take your grandma over to the well and get her some water or she'll never leave."

As Granny pushed on the stair step with a wrinkled old hand, her arm shaking like the legs on a newborn calf, she muttered something about having to go find another hobo. I stayed on the porch because I wanted to hear what Momma and Walker said.

"What about those men?" Momma asked him. "You think you could shoot them if they came around?"

"I wouldn't want it to come to that, ma'am."

She said, "That ain't what I asked you, mister."

Looking down, shifting his weight from one foot to the other like a boy asking a girl to dance for the first time, the stranger said, "I haven't got a gun."

"Well I do, and I'm asking you again. You gonna shoot them if they come around?"

He cleared his throat and spit in the dirt. "It'd be me against a bunch of them, wouldn't it?"

After taking a deep breath, the way she did when Daddy made her mad, she asked him, "Why's it so hard to get an answer out of you?"

"Sometimes you do something you know is wrong, just 'cause you don't have time to think on it."

Momma shook her head. "If that means you'll help us if trouble comes, you can go make yourself a place in the barn."

He stepped back, said, "Ma'am" then put his hat on and headed down the hill toward the barn.

Momma nudged me again. "Go on child. Help your grandma get her drink."

I found Granny around back struggling to turn the crank handle on our well. She might be taller than me, but I'm a lot stronger, so I did it for her.

After sipping from the ladle she said, "I worry what's gonna come of you out here all alone with that sinful woman."

Her dark eyes staring at me over the rim of the cup made me uncomfortable. I was glad when she'd had her drink and started for home. I ran back around the house and hopped onto the porch just as Walker disappeared into the barn. Wrapping my arms around Momma's waist, I asked her if he was going to stay.

Momma hugged me real tight so I knew something was

worrying her. When I asked her what was wrong, she said, "I hope letting that man stay wasn't a mistake. I hope he doesn't just eat our food and run off at the first sign of trouble."

As I lay awake late into the night, with not even a hint of a breeze coming through my window to relieve the sticky night air, I imagined Walker living in some far-away place. And that he had a daughter and they lived in a grand house and had nice things. And every night he would sit on his daughter's bed and read to her. And when he kissed her good-night, she knew he'd always be there, so she wasn't ever scared.

And I imagined that something terrible had happened, his daughter and his wife both dying; maybe from the same sickness that came through here last year, like the plagues we learned about in bible school. It killed all kinds of people around here, including aunt Bella and two of my cousins.

I imagined Walker riding the rails to get away from all that sadness then falling in love with Momma and staying. Then I'd never have to be scared again. But it was just make-believe, and because, deep down, I knew that, I didn't sleep well.

When I woke the next morning, the weak yellow light of early dawn was coming through a crack in my curtains and shining on the old rag dolls across the room on my dresser. My two rag dolls had been my Momma's when she was little, and that's all the dolls I have. Momma says we can't afford dolls now that Daddy's gone.

But Granny has a big cupboard full of dolls with pretty painted faces, and a box full of dresses and shoes and hats to put on them. I got up and ran out to the kitchen where I found Momma bent over the table kneading bread dough.

"Can I go to Granny's house, Momma? Please, Momma, can I?"

She stopped what she was doing and frowned at me. "I don't like you going over there."

"But I'm almost the marrying age, Momma."

"You're barely eleven years old, child,"

"Please, Momma."

Momma wiped her hands on her apron. She came over to me and knelt down, putting her hands on my shoulders, forcing me to look at her. "You can go there after your chores are done, but only if you do a good job of them."

Then she shook me gently and told me, "But don't you believe a single thing that old witch says about me, do you hear?"

"Oh no ma'am," I said, shaking my head, "I won't believe a word of it."

I left for Granny's house right after lunch wearing my Sunday dress and my Sunday shoes. But before I left, I washed my hands and my face and brushed my hair, 'cause Granny says little girls should always be clean and neat. Mommy put my hair up on my head in a big swirl and put my pretty painted hairpin in it to hold it in place.

You're wondering how Momma could afford to give me a painted hairpin. Well, after Daddy left us, Momma wouldn't wear anything he'd given her. But that pin was just too pretty to throw away so she gave it to me instead.

The day had turned out grand, with a breeze from the north that smelled of wildflowers keeping me cool as I walked over the hill to Granny's. On the way up the hill I picked a daisy and chanted, "He loves her; he loves her not," as I pulled the petals off. When I saw that the game would end wrong; with Walker not loving Momma, I picked a different daisy.

At the top of the hill I stopped. Sometimes I climbed the hill just to look at the view, because from there I could see the edge of the world, a world of wondrous places that I would see someday by following the road that started in front of Granny's house.

From there on the hilltop I saw two tiny figures sitting on her front porch; Granny and a man dressed all in black like the preacher at our Sunday service. I thought about going back home because of the man, but then I thought, "Gee, with him there Granny might let me play with her good china dolls all by myself," so I started down the hill.

Granny's house looked like a fairytale palace compared

to the little house Momma and I lived in. Her big white porch gleaming so bright in the sun that it almost hurt to look at it, stretched all the way across the front of her big three-story house. She's always bragging that it's Queen Anne. I don't know what that means but I remember it because it's Momma's name too, and if my life was a fairytale, Momma would be a queen and we'd live in a great white castle.

The man dressed in black spotted me when I was about half-way down the hill. I knew he did because he pointed at me. He reminded me of my uncle Jim, who says he's thirty-something, and who, according to Momma, hasn't ever done a lick of work.

When I got close enough to hear what they were saying I stopped. The man smiled at me, but there was no kindness in it, and he said a strange thing, the way grownups say things when they don't really want you to answer them. "What miracle is this that God hath wrought? I did nearly mistake that golden hair for an angel's halo."

I don't like grownups talking about me like that, pretending I'm not there when they can see me plain as day.

Granny told the man, "There's no need to spoil the child. Her mother's already done a passable job of that," which wasn't true. I wasn't spoiled, not one bit.

The man stood and leaned against a porch post. With the sun in my eyes, and him way up there on the porch dressed all in black, his face appeared to float above me like in a nightmare.

And he talked funny, making his words sound more dramatic than they should, the way Momma talked when she read me a fairytale. "Can this dear, sweet child be the same troubled girl you told me about?"

First Granny told the man she was worried about my soul, whatever that means, then she told him, "Lord knows what she's learning from her tramp of a mother."

That really made me mad because I know what the word "tramp" means. I know because I asked Mamma what it means when I heard someone call my Aunt Laura a tramp. So I told

Granny not to talk about my momma that way, but she didn't seem to hear me.

As I walked the last few feet to Granny's porch steps the man's eyes followed me like an angry dog's glare. Then he held both his arms out in a grand gesture and told my granny, "Surely, ma'am, convincing a simple country woman to accept God's truth should be easy for a woman who runs a place as substantial as this."

I stomped my foot to get Granny's attention, but it didn't do any good.

Granny told the man, "I'd be grateful, sir, if you took a personal interest in this girl and her mother. You being a preacher and all."

"I will do precisely that," the man said. "I will do it for the sake of this lovely child."

I don't know why Granny would sic a strange preacher man on Momma and me, but I didn't like it one bit. And to get them to stop talking about me like I wasn't there, I yelled, "Hey."

When Granny told me to shush I started up the steps. If they were going to be mean I was going to go play with her dolls.

But when I got up on the porch Granny stepped in front of me. "And just where do you think you're going, child?"

When I tried get around her she blocked my way with one of her bony arms.

While I did a little dance hoping to get around Granny, the preacher asked her, "You told me that the girl and her mother are alone, did you not?"

After stepping into the doorway to block me, Granny put her hands on her chest as though she'd gotten some terrible news. But she didn't fool me 'cause I'd seen her do that before.

Then she started in on my momma again, saying, "That woman's wickedness was too much for my poor son, devoted as he was. And now she's alone and in need of spiritual guidance such as you could give her."

fix "Then I will go see her this very day," he said, talking solemnly, the way people do at a funeral.

When Granny said, "You have lifted a great burden from these devout but frail little shoulders," the man in black didn't see her grin because he was staring at me.

Bowing slightly, the preacher said to Granny, "Someday I will tell you stories that will lighten your heart, but this day passes quickly so I should be on my way. Now, if you'd write a short letter of introduction for me to give your daughter-in-law our chances for a successful outcome might be assured."

I tried to tell Granny to stop, that they were scaring me, but she put a finger to her lips warning me to be quiet then went inside, closing the door behind her, leaving me there with that preacher. If didn't believe in the boogeyman when I was little, it's because I'd never met this man.

When Granny came out, she handed him a piece of paper. He smiled and bowed slightly when he took it from her then stepped off the porch.

Granny took me by the hand and led me down the steps. Then she bent down and put her wrinkly face so close to mine I could see the little hairs in her nose. She did it to scare me, so I'd do what she told me, which was. "You be a good girl and take the preacher to see your momma."

The man came to me and put his hand out. I backed away from him until I could turn around and run on ahead without him grabbing me. Granny yelled at me to stop, but I ran as fast as I could all the way to the top of the hill. From there I looked back hoping to see the man still at Granny's house, but he was already half way up the hill.

I ran as fast as I could down the hill toward my house, all the time yelling, "Momma, come quick."

Stepping out of the kitchen door just as I got there, she asked, "What's wrong, child?"

I wrapped my arms around her, hiding my face in the folds of her dress, panting hard but feeling safe. Peeking out from behind her I pointed at the man coming down the hill. "That man's bringing trouble, Momma."

She asked what he'd done to me.

"Nothing, Momma. But he talks funny like our Sunday preacher, and he and Granny said things I didn't like.

By then, the man was close enough to hear what Momma said to him without her having to yell. "You can stop right there, mister."

But he didn't stop, not until he got so close he could touch Momma. Then, holding the piece of paper Granny gave him out toward Momma, he told her, "I have a note here from Mrs. Scott."

Momma must've expected trouble because she pushed me behind her. Then she put her hands on her hips and told the man she didn't care if the note was from God, she wanted him to leave.

The preacher told Momma he wasn't going anywhere, and that, "The Lord teaches us to open our hearts and our homes to the less fortunate."

"You don't look like one of the less fortunate."

He frowned as he put the note from Granny in his bible, then told Momma, "Mrs. Scott believes that you have lost your way."

"How lost can I be standing on my doorstep?"

He dropped his bible. That startled Momma. She looked down at it. Fast as an angry snake, his hand shot out and grabbed her. Momma tried to twist free, but with one hand over her mouth and the preacher's other hand around her waist, he dragged her into the house.

I ran to the barn to get Walker. I found him hoeing weeds in the field out back of it. I wrapped my arms around his waist while I tried to get my breath back from the running and crying.

"Whoa there, girl," he said, kneeling down so he could look me in the eyes.

Momma screamed. Walker told me to hide in the barn then ran toward the house. I followed him - I was too scared to be by myself. We fund them in Momma's bedroom. The preacher had her on the bed.

As Walker went for a rifle leaning in the corner of the room the preacher got off the bed. He lunged at Walker. Walker hit him with the butt of the rifle. The preacher stumbled backward, grabbing the doorframe to steady himself. Blood trickled from the gash on his head.

Slurring the words, "You'll regret this," he staggered out of the room.

Walker followed him out, with Momma right behind him, and me right behind her. When I got to the back door Walker was standing outside watching the preacher walk up the hill. Momma was watching from the doorway. I wrapped my arms around her legs. The preacher stopped to look at us before he started down the other side of the hill.

When he was out of sight Momma asked Walker why he didn't shoot the preacher.

"It's not enough that he's gone?"

"No it's not," she said, shaking her head, "because now I have to worry about him coming back."

I wished Momma hadn't said that 'cause now I'd be too scared to sleep thinking about the preacher coming back.

After making a show of yanking on the rifle bolt, Walker said to Momma, "Gun's jammed."

"Can you fix it?"

He held the rifle close and looked inside it. All he said was, "Maybe," but I knew he could, and I knew he'd shoot the preacher if the preacher ever came back. I was sure of it.

Walker nodded his head toward the hill. "Do you want me to follow him, make sure he doesn't hurt your mother?"

"That old witch ain't my mother."

"Just the same, he might hurt her."

"Let him," Momma said, "she's the one who sent him here."

He tipped his head, said, "Ma'am" then headed toward the barn.

I was wishing he and Momma got along better when she asked me if I still said my prayers every night. I nodded my head.

"Well, tonight I want you to pray for Walker to kill that man if he comes back."

"But Momma, at Bible school they taught us we shouldn't

pray for things like that."

She told me to take off my good clothes. As I walked away she asked me, "What's the point in praying if you can't pray for what you need?"

I tried playing with my dolls, but no amount of make-believe could put the world back the way it was before the preacher showed up. So I helped Momma make bread. I did most of the kneading, which is really hard work. After that I sat on the front steps and made pictures in the dirt while it baked, the smell making my stomach growl for a piece of it hot out of the oven.

I'd eaten near half a loaf of it when Momma gave me a new loaf wrapped in a towel and told me to take it out to Walker. "And long as you're going, you might as well take this too." She handed me a little cardboard box that was very heavy. I ran toward the barn. She yelled, "No dallying. You come right back."

Our barn was built into the hillside with big sliding doors, so wagons loaded with hay from the harvest could be pulled into the upstairs loft for unloading. There was still some old hay scattered about the loft but the stalls below had been empty of animals ever since my daddy left. Momma told me she had to sell them so we could eat the winter he left.

I slid one of the big loft doors open far enough to slip in sideways, the musty smell of old hay filling my nose, the dry dusty air nearly causing a coughing spell. Tiptoeing quiet as a mouse over to the trap door where Daddy threw hay down to the cow, I opened it slowly so the hinges wouldn't squeak.

Walker was sitting on a wooden crate below me. Daddy's rifle was leaning against the wall next to him and there was another crate in front of him with some pieces of the gun on it. As I watched him wiping things with a rag, the familiar smell of oil drifted up through the trap door, reminding me of daddy.

Even though I sat down very carefully, I still knocked some hay into the hole, which floated down to Walker like snowflakes.

And even though he didn't look up, I knew he'd seen

them because he stopped what he was doing to ask, "Does your momma know you're out here?"

I held the box Momma gave me out over the opening so he could see it. "I brought you a loaf of bread and this."

Looking up at me through the opening he said, "That's a dangerous place to sit, missy."

I told him I'd done it lots of times.

He pulled an empty crate over next to him and gave it a pat. "Why don't you come down here and sit?"

I ran outside and around the end of the barn to the door on the lower level. Sitting on the crate next to him I watched him rub a funny looking little piece of metal with a rag then hold it up to the lantern to inspect it.

"Will you shoot that man if he comes back?" I asked, hoping he'd say 'yes' so I wouldn't have to worry about the preacher.

He took a deep breath and his hands went limp in his lap. Then he looked at me and frowned. "Killing's a sin, young lady."

I asked him if it was always a sin.

"That's what the Good Book says."

"No matter how bad a person is?"

"I reckon killing is killing, no matter why you do it."

I told him it wasn't fair.

He picked up another piece of the gun. As he rubbed it with the rag he said, "Let's talk about something else, shall we?"

So I asked him if he liked my momma. He stopped what he was doing and sat very still so I had to wait for his answer.

I almost fell off the crate when Momma shouted from right behind me, "Didn't I tell you to come right back?" then grabbed me by the hand and yanked me to my feet.

Her voice was still trembling and very loud when she yelled at Walker. "I don't want you filling her head with silliness."

All Walker said to her was, "Ma'am."

At first Momma just stared at him all red faced and breathing hard, like Granny was after walking over the hill. But she didn't stay mad very long. I could tell because she stopped squeezing my hand so hard it hurt.

She squinted at Walker, said, "The work is hard and hot and I can't pay you? So why do you stay?"

"I won't talk to the girl if you don't want me to."

She let out a slow, tired-sounding sigh. "Walker, or whatever your name is, you've got a maddening way of not answering me."

He held a piece of the gun up toward the glow of the lantern. "I like seeing new places. Places where everything's different, and not just the people, but the weather, and the shapes the stars make, and the color of the dirt under my boots, even the sounds the bugs make."

She asked him how long he planned to stay, but instead of answering, he told her, "That old woman was right, you know. Those men might come looking for you."

"How are they gonna find out about us, hidden behind the hill like we are?"

"One of your neighbors will tell them. And it's because you're hidden and can't get help that they'll come here."

"And why would one of my neighbor's tell them about us?"

"Because those men are gonna threaten some woman's family and she's gonna tell them about you to save her own. So you need to think about what's gonna happen when they get here."

"I already did. That's why I let you stay. And that gun you're cleaning; that's what it's for."

"But there'll be a bunch of them and they'll likely have guns too. One old man with a rifle isn't gonna scare them."

"I don't want you to scare them. I want you to kill them."

He didn't say a thing. He just looked at her.

"You got a problem with that?" Momma asked, daring him to say yes.

"Unrealistic expectations get people killed, ma'am."

That made Momma so angry she squeezed my hand until it hurt. "Don't talk to me about unrealistic," she said, "I'm raising a child in this God-forsaken place."

After that Momma practically dragged me back to the house then told me to get to bed. But I didn't fall asleep until very late, worrying that the preacher would come back, and wondering what Walker would do if he did.

Late the next afternoon after my chores were done I sat on the back steps and watched a giant red evening sun disappear behind the hill, my empty stomach making noises because I smelled biscuits baking.

I was wondering how I could get Walker and my mother to like each other when I noticed lights flashing on the clouds. It meant a car was coming, its headlights pointed at the sky as it climbed the other side of the hill between our house and Granny's. I waited and watched, and listened to the car's engine struggle.

When the car appeared as a black shape silhouetted against the red sky at the top of the hill, I yelled for Momma. A moment later she came outside. "Go find Walker," she said, "and hurry, child."

I ran fast as the wind. When I came out of the barn with Walker, I saw three men standing outside our kitchen door with granny Scott. When we got closer, I saw that the biggest one talking to Momma had a shiny star on his shirt and I heard him tell Momma, "He's coming back with us, lady. And if you give me any trouble, I'll throw you in the cell next to him."

When Momma pleaded with the man he nodded toward Granny and said, "He stole from her so I've gotta take him in."

The other two men grabbed Walker by both arms and led him to the car. I tugged on Momma's dress and pleaded with her to do something. She pulled my hand away then walked to the car where Granny was sitting in back seat with her window down.

The big man started the car but before he drove away Momma yelled to him, "Walker couldn't have stolen from her. He never left here."

After the car had disappeared over the hill Momma told

me to go inside.

I stomped my foot and shouted. "You just let them take Walker from us."

"Wasn't a thing I could do," she said. "Besides he's just a drifter."

Fighting back tears, I told her, "You let him go, just like you did with Papa."

Then I ran because I knew Momma would be mad at me for saying that.

She yelled, "You come back here, child," but I ran around the side of the house.

I sat on the ground behind the well to hide from Momma and wondered what would happen to Walker. I wondered if he'd ever come back, and wondered if the preacher would come back while he was gone.

I think I'd been there a long time when I saw headlights shining on the clouds again and heard another car fighting its way up the hill. I ran to tell Momma, but she must have heard it already because she was standing in the kitchen doorway when I got there.

When she told me, "You wait here for me, child," she sounded frantic, which scared me even more than her leaving me there alone.

By the time she came out of the barn carrying the gun the car had reached the top of the hill and started down toward our house. Momma met me at the kitchen door just as headlights flooded the back of our house with a bright light as harsh as a lightening flash. She pulled me inside then pushed me into to the far corner of the kitchen and stood in front of me as she fumbled with the gun trying to put bullets in it. I asked her if it was the bad men.

"Hush, child," she told me.

I knew she was scared too - I felt her hand shaking. Then the car lights went out and everything got quiet. I held my breath. I heard a car door open and close then two more.

Someone appeared in the doorway, a black shape in the

white glare of the headlights. Momma fired the gun. The man in the doorway staggered backwards right out of the kitchen. The noise stole my breath and made my ears ring. The smell of gunpowder filled the room.

While Momma fumbled with the bolt on the gun I heard angry talk outside. "I ain't about to get shot. It's my car. I'm leaving. You can come with me or you can go to hell."

I heard a gunshot outside. A man yelled, "You hear that lady? It's just you and me now," and I knew the voice. The preacher was back.

Momma whispered to me, "If something happens to me, you run and hide in the woods, and you stay there until he's gone."

I clutched her skirt with both hands and told myself that nothing would happen to her, because I couldn't think about being alone with the preacher.

I heard his voice again, but this time it was at the front door, on the other side of the house. "I suppose you already figured out that I'm not really a preacher. But you gotta admit it was a hell of an idea. It's surprising what people will tell a man of the cloth, surprising how easy it is to find out where the easy pickings are."

For a while all I heard were crickets in the fields around the house. Then the preacher's voice punched through the darkness again. "I knew you and the girl would be alone out here tonight. You wanna know how I knew that?"

I heard him doing something out front, but I couldn't tell what. Then he yelled, "Maybe you don't want to know, but I'm gonna tell you anyway. After your hobo attacked me, I convinced the old hag to tell the sheriff he stole from her. Then I watched the sheriff's office until they brought him in. And now it's my will that'll be done."

From where we were hiding in the kitchen I could see the front door. It opened a crack and the preacher set something down on the floor inside. A small flame glowed brightly for a moment then pulsed faintly. I waited and watched.

It exploded. The brightness hurt my eyes. Hot dry air hit my face. My ears rang. Momma pulled me hard, out the back door. The preacher was there waiting for us. He knocked Momma down.

She yelled, "Run."

I ran, all the way to the barn then squeezed through the loft doors. When I peeked back at the house through a crack in the siding I couldn't see Momma or the preacher. If Momma didn't get away from him, I'd be on my own. Then I'd need to hide. With no moonlight the woods were much too dark and scary. If I hid in the barn, he'd find me eventually. And I couldn't run to Granny's house because she's the one who sent the preacher to us.

Then I remembered something Walker had said to me. I went back outside and stood in front of the loft doors to wait for the preacher. I think I watched the house for an eternity, feeling God awful scared the whole time, and even more scared when the preacher came out of the house carrying a lantern. When he held it up the light swept across the field to find me.

Grinning like a crazy man, he yelled, "I'm gonna teach you a hard lesson, little girl," then came after me.

Shaking uncontrollably like my Granny I watched him come for me. What had seemed like a good idea before, now seemed stupid and hopeless, but it was too late to do anything different. So I waited until his hand was barely a foot away before I spun around to squeeze between the loft doors.

But I'd waited too long. He caught the sleeve of my dress and pulled, hard, almost pulling me to him until the sleeve tore. I got free then and slipped inside inside the barn. He came after me but couldn't get through the narrow opening. He grunted. The hinges creaked as he pushed the heavy doors open.

He held the lantern up, caught me in its glare. We were separated by a space no bigger than a door mat. He grinned at me took a step closer. I stepped back. He lunged, tried to grab me then fell through the straw I had spread over the open trapdoor.

Letting go of the lantern, he put his hands out to catch the trapdoor frame. I stomped on one of them as hard as I could. He let go, fell through the opening. I kicked the lantern into the hole.

I soon saw a soft fluttering glow in the opening. I leaned over the edge to look. The preacher lay crumpled on the plough below, like a discarded rag doll, with the broken lantern next to him. Thick gray smoke rose from it. Then the hay burst into flames.

I ran from the barn. On the way to the house I heard him scream. By then the whole front of our house was in flames. I found Momma tied up on the floor of the kitchen. I used a kitchen knife to cut her loose.

When we got outside she asked if I was hurt.

"No, Momma."

She asked me where the preacher was.

"He's in the barn. He burned up."

I leaned in against Momma's waist and closed my eyes and held on tight. With the preacher gone I was safe.

Then I felt Momma's body tense. I peeked out from behind her skirt. Like our house, the barn was in flames. I watched a dark shape stagger toward us out of the billowing smoke. The preacher was back.

Momma pulled my arms from around her waist and told me to wait there. I held on to her with all my might and begged her not to leave me.

She pulled my arms free then got down on one knee. Squeezing my arms so hard it hurt she told me, "Do as I say, child. I have to end this."

She left me to watch the preacher, who was so close I could see blackened skin on his face oozing blood like a hog cooking over a fire pit. He staggered, but kept coming, the space between us no bigger than the length of my bed. I stepped back. He would've reached me if I hadn't. I wondered what was keeping Momma. He reached for me.

Momma stepped between us. The preacher grinned at her and kept coming. She shot him. He staggered but didn't fall.

Momma hit him in the head with the rifle butt so hard his head flopped over like a broken doll. He slumped to his knees right in front of her. Momma worked the bolt then held the gun to his chest and shot him. He fell and didn't move. She threw the empty gun at him.

Then she reached for my hand. "Come on, child, let's go see about your grandma."

At the top of the hill I stopped to look back at the house where I'd grown up. There was nothing left but its skeleton. I ran to catch up with Momma.

Granny's front door was wide open. Inside it was dark and silent. We found Granny hiding in a closet, sitting on the floor with her knees pulled up to her chest and tears streaming down her face. She asked Momma where the preacher was.

"I killed him."

When Momma reached for Granny, Granny shook her head and tried to shrink away. Momma told her to get up.

Whimpering like a little girl, Grammy said, "I didn't know he was one of them."

Momma grabbed her by the arm and yanked her to her feet. "We're staying in town tonight, and you're coming with us because you've got money and I don't."

Momma pushed Granny ahead of her, toward the front door. "Tomorrow morning we're going to the bank, and you're gonna give me back the money we paid you for that no-good piece of land you sold us. Then we're going to see the sheriff. And after you tell him Walker didn't steal from you, Eve and I are going someplace far away."

I tugged on Momma's dress. "Can Walker come with us, Momma?"

"If he wants to."

I knew he would. I just knew it.

WHEN GOOD FOOD
GOES BAD

W hen I got to the crime scene the medical examiner was kneeling on the floor next to the victim, poking around in a cavernous hole where the poor slob's stomach should've been. And judging from the guy's injuries, he'd been killed by just the sort of doomsday thing I'm paid to watch for but hope I never find.

And as luck would have it, that's where I met the girl of my dreams after bumbling through life for thirty odd years alone. All I had to do to save her life, and the lives of everyone else I knew, was convince her that her instincts were wrong and that life itself was on brink of extinction.

I learned about the dead man early this morning while working on my weekly status report when Josh, our techie who monitors the communications passing between several other government agencies, yelled, "Got one, Ron," from his cubicle across the room.

I hurried over to his desk to ask him why he thought it was an event.

"Because," he said, "according to the cop who called it in, most of the victim's midsection was missing. He said it looked like an explosive device had gone off in the guy's stomach."

Brenda, our receptionist, had heard Josh call to me and

joined us, the resulting commotion getting the attention of our boss, Dennis, who made a rare and unwelcomed appearance. He came out of his office and headed our way, yelling, "If you people don't have enough work, I can make more staff cuts."

When Dennis demanded, "What the hell's going on?" Brenda, bless her heart, tried to distract him with a lie. "I'm taking donations for John's wife. She had a baby yesterday."

Shaking his head, Dennis spun around, poked me in the chest and said, "In my office," then told the others to get back to work.

I had a pretty good idea what to expect and knew I wouldn't like it, but did as I was told because I need the job. I followed him into his office, closing the door behind us then stood awkwardly in front of his desk while I waited for him to sit down.

Dennis cleared his throat, which was no doubt a warning to me to pay attention. "I haven't seen this week's status report yet, so I know you've got something better to do than waste your time on whatever that nonsense was out there."

I never tell him any more than I have to, so I said, "Suspicious death," and left it at that.

"I don't care what it is," he said, waving his hand dismissively. "But if this is another one of your wild goose chases and the press gets word of it I'll have your job and your pension."

Hoping to avoid a lengthy discussion because I wanted to get to the crime scene before forensics hauled the victim's body away, I told him, "No problem," and tried to sound sincere. Then I headed for the door hoping he was done with me.

He said, "Hey, I'm not done with you."

I stopped at the door, twisting around to look back at him, but kept left my hand on the doorknob so I'd be ready for a quick exit when I got another chance. He tapped his pencil on his desk blotter angrily and stared at me. His blood pressure rose visibly whenever one of us left the office, because according to him it afforded us, "An opportunity to make him angry by doing something stupid."

Unfortunately our job didn't get us out of the office much, because annoying him was one of the job's few perks.

"How many times do I have to explain this to you?" he asked. "This bioengineering disaster stuff is just a bunch of scientific sounding bullshit someone dreamed up to scare Congress into funding us. If anybody actually believed it they would've made us part of Homeland Security."

Dennis' version of what happened conveniently leaves out most of what really happened, like Congress creating our department because of some dire predictions made by a group of academics at one of their hearings. After which a frightened Congress set us up as a special branch of the FDA, and charged us with regulating new bio-engineered food additives.

Congress meant well, but it hasn't worked out well because the food industry began funneling truckloads of money into congressional campaign coffers. So now when Congress funds our agency it's with the proviso that we won't disrupt the flow of money by angering the food producers. And to ensure that wouldn't happen, Congress put a disbeliever in charge of us.

I wanted to confront him with the truth - that he was worried more about disruptions to his income than he was about the public's welfare, but to avoid a lecture I assured him I'd be discrete. Then I opened the door to leave, because as far as I was concerned our meeting was over.

"I'm warning you," he said, shaking a finger at me.

As I closed the door I heard, "I swear you'll be outta here if the press gets word of this."

Even though I was in a hurry, I stopped at Josh's cubicle to praise him for intercepting the communication about the possible event.

Chico, the guy in the cubicle next to Josh, overheard us and stood up to talk to me over the cubicle wall. "Hey, Ron, we're ordering takeout from Danny's Grill. You interested?"

The same five cheapskates had lunch delivered two or three times a week, and Chico was the cheapest of the lot. I handed him three twenty dollar bills. "I'll buy and you can keep the change, but only if it's from LingLing's."

I'd been dying for some of LingLing's sweet and sour chicken. Just thinking about it made me salivate. For me, food had always been a vice, but lately LingLing's had become an addiction. The large helping I ingested two or three times a week would no doubt ensure my early demise, but living without it would be like a death sentence.

Even though I risked getting a traffic ticket on my way to the crime scene it was still twenty minutes later when I turned down a narrow side street lined with low-rent brownstones. Two double-parked police cars and an ambulance, all with their lights flashing, had traffic blocked in both directions. The crime scene tape, strung haphazardly all over the neighborhood, looked like a giant yellow cobweb.

I showed my badge to get through the clog of uniforms and civilians milling about on the sidewalk then took the stairs to the victim's second floor apartment. Although the place had seen better days, the tattered condition of the furniture was nothing compared to the state of the victim, an overweight middle-aged man with a round fleshy face, pudgy nose, and wispy blond hair. His body, what was left of it, was slumped in a badly stained and nearly threadbare recliner.

A man in a white lab coat, who I assumed was the ME, was kneeling on the floor next to the victim. Built like an ant, with an oversize head held precariously above his narrow shoulders by a pencil-thin neck, the man needed to be put on a regimen of steroids, free-weights, and fatty foods.

With his face hovering just inches from the cavity in the dead man's stomach, he used a pencil to poke at the grisly pile of internal organs in the victim's lap. As I walked around the recliner to get a better look, two things became obvious immediately: I didn't have the stomach for something this gruesome, and we had an event on our hands.

"What happened to him?" I asked as casually as I could, while silently vowing never to eat again.

His head snapped around and he focused two bright-green

eyes on me, then he made a face at me and stood up. I spotted a fresh-looking smudge of bloody viscera on his lab coat, and afraid it could be harboring a microscopic man-eater, I pointed at it. "You've got some of the victim on you."

"Who the hell are you?" he asked.

I stepped back, because I was worried about the goo on his coat even if he wasn't. I flashed my badge at him, but did it quickly so he wouldn't have time to read it. I have yet to meet someone who's intimidated by a badge with the Food and Drug Administration's insignia on it.

It's real enough but no one takes it seriously, and who can blame them; it's not as though we could actually arrest anyone, and most people don't live in fear of their name appearing on an FDA report.

Luckily for me he didn't look closely at it. Apparently he thought I was just another one of the federal agents who routinely got in his way, because he went back to examining the victim and ignoring me.

Just then a thirtyish woman sporting a young girl's haircut burst into the apartment wearing a snug-fitting pantsuit that looked so good on her I think its designer would've been surprised. Even without makeup or jewelry she looked so good I couldn't help staring. When she pretended to cough I realized my eyes had been lingering where they shouldn't have, and I felt the heat on my face as I blushed.

She eyed me warily, asking, "What's the story here, Jack?" as she approached me.

Even though she'd been looking at me, I had assumed 'Jack' was the name of the ME kneeling by the victim, and that her question had been directed at him. I was wrong.

Getting up close and in my face, she said, "I asked you a question."

I held my badge up.

She snatched it out of my hand, and studying it like an alien artifact, said, "You want to tell me what you're doing on my turf?"

I thought she should've introduced herself, as a professional courtesy, and I told her so.

She smiled and said, "Detective Blanchard," but it was a small, tight smile and not particularly friendly. "Now how about telling me what you're doing at my crime scene?"

I led her by the arm to the other side of the room so the ME wouldn't hear me, because it's tough enough convincing one disbeliever that life-threatening, cannibalistic microorganisms exist, forget convincing two of them.

I recited the official version of our group's mission. "I work for a special branch of the FDA that was set up to oversee the development and deployment of engineered food additives."

With her tightly closed lips twitching slightly, as though she was suppressing a laugh, she tipped her head a little to the side and said loud enough for the ME to hear, "Is this some kind of joke?"

When I told her, "For thousands of years, people have used spices to disguise the stench of spoiled meat," she snickered and said, "So you think that guy in there was attacked by a foul-smelling steak?"

As if her devilish grin didn't make her attractive enough, she'd fixed her stunning blue eyes on me while she poked fun at me. It was nice change from the Sergeant Friday types I usually got stuck with. But I feared this incident could be the real thing and I needed her to take the threat seriously. Hoping a microscopic invader wouldn't seem so fantastic if she knew how it got there, I gave her a quick history lesson.

"One day a group of well-intentioned cerebral types developed some non-natural food additives, and life got better for the consumer. The next big breakthrough came when someone realized that by properly marketing the additives they could significantly increase food sales, and they could do so without incurring the exorbitant costs associated with actually improving the food. The profits earned by the companies selling the additives were staggering."

"What the hell?" she said, shaking her pretty head.

I'm used to skepticism. It's an occupational hazard. So I just forged ahead. "But they'd unleashed a monster. The food industry told the public it was nano-technology, a modern marvel that promised all kinds of miracles, most of it unsubstantiated hype carefully worded to avoid future lawsuits. But with billions of dollars at stake, food additives are already being tested; additives they claim can scrub the cholesterol from our arteries and dissolve unwanted fat. And if that sounds too good to be true, it is. Because fueled by risky science and insatiable greed they're creating microscopic life forms that can be lethal, life forms that have no natural predators and can reproduce at staggering exponential rates."

She stared at me, grimacing as though she'd eaten something that hadn't agreed with her.

But I didn't let her skepticism faze me. I'm made of tougher stuff than that. "When the scientific community found out about this they lobbied Congress. An alarmed Agriculture Committee established our group."

She opened her mouth to say something, but only got one unintelligible syllable out before she closed it again. She no doubt thought I was nuts, but she didn't walk away. I took that as a good sign.

So I went ahead with the lesson, all the while wishing there was something I could say to get her as interested in me as she was in the dead man. "It's my job to monitor the production of bio-engineered substances. And when a problem is reported, it's my job to prevent it from becoming a doomsday event."

She blinked and said, "A what?"

"In layman's terms, that guy in there ate something he shouldn't have and it chewed a big hole in him."

"You know what I think?" she said. "I think your science fiction is more fiction than science."

I told her that the thought of something escaping from one of the research labs terrified me.

That earned me a smile along with another wisecrack. "Tell me, do you chase rogue recipe ingredients too, or just fugitive food additives? Jesus, that's almost as hard to say as it is to believe."

If I was right about the guy in the next room- that he'd been done in by a lethal lab accident, detective Blanchard and I could be its next victims, followed by everyone else on the planet. Sad to think the most fun I'd ever had with a woman was trying to convince Blanchard of our imminent doom. Already I didn't want anything to happen to her. I wanted to get to know her better, to spend time with her without a dead body present, like normal people do.

"Think about it," I told her. "A bunch of greedy investors hire some kids with more college degrees than sense to develop a new life form. Those over-educated lab-coats design a molecular-sized robot to eat the cholesterol out of our arteries. And because the approval process is expensive and the company wants to be sure that it'll be profitable, it runs trials on mass-producing the stuff before it's been approved.

"It's a statistical certainty that they'll eventually produce a defective batch. And the lab assistants actually working with the stuff are all too often high school dropouts or illegal aliens who have no idea what they're handling. With the naked eye a bad batch doesn't look any different than any other batch. And they'd never know it if they accidently cross-contaminated an additive that's being used on a food production line in the same factory."

She said, "That sounds like the plot from one of those 'B' movies they made back in the fifties, the ones with frightened girls wearing tight sweaters."

She touched my forehead, said, "I think you might have a short circuit up there."

I wasn't sure where my eyes had been, but I do remember trying to imagine her in a tight sweater. If I'd been staring inappropriately, she was good-natured about it- my kind of girl. I wondered if she had a husband or kids. "What if it gets into the breakfast cereal your son wolfs down before he goes to school?"

"Nice try," she said, "but I don't have a kid."

"Then pretend it was your husband's cereal."

"Even if I had one, it wouldn't be any of your business."

She had such an odd way about her, but I couldn't help liking it. And anyway, I'd found out what I wanted to know – that she was single.

She handed back my badge and told me, "If you stay out of my way, and you don't touch anything, I won't arrest you. And keep this to yourself. I don't care if people think you're nuts, but I don't want anybody thinking I believe your nonsense."

Having dismissed me as harmless, she turned her attention to the ME, crossing the room to hover over him while he inspected the victim. "And what have we here?"

Glancing up from the pile of visceral goo in the dead guy's lap the ME said, "Intestines," rather matter-of-factly. It may have been an attempt at humor.

"Yeah, I figured that much out on my own," she said. "What I'd like to know is what happened to him. You think you could help me out with that?"

I hoped to hear a plausible explanation for the condition of the deceased, one that wouldn't require my services. Instead, the ME told Blanchard the guy was supposed to meet a friend, and that when he didn't show, the friend came looking for him. It was the friend who called 911.

"And that's the way his friend found him," detective Blanchard asked, "with that big nasty hole in him?"

After focusing his disturbing green eyes on her, he told her, "This is the strangest stiff I've ever seen," and judging from the ME's bald head and the deep creases on his face, med school was a distant memory for him. So I figured he'd probably seen some pretty weird stuff.

"And by strange you mean what exactly?" she asked.

"Think about what it would take to do this kind of damage. Then think about the fact that this guy had his shirt on when I got here, and that it was intact and buttoned, soaked with blood but intact. You tell me, what kind of nut job would take off someone's shirt and do this, then put the guy's shirt back on and button it up?"

Blanchard said, "Druggies," as though the one word explained everything.

The ME shook his head. "That does not begin to explain this."

With a big grin she nodded her head in my direction and told him, "This guy thinks a rogue food additive made a break for it by tunneling its way out of the guy's stomach."

It earned me a derisive smile from the ME, after which detective Blanchard offered us her theory. "The gangs that run the drugs in this town can be real creative, especially when it comes to killing off their rivals. I figure someone was muscling in on someone else's turf and this mess is a warning to back off."

The woman sure was pigheaded, but in an attractive way. I assumed she'd seen so many drug-related crimes that any other motive seemed improbable to her. But I can be just as pigheaded. And something had been bothering me about the victim, so I took a long hard look at him.

After my stomach had done a few cartwheels I spotted the problem. "Look as his ribs. Does he look like your typical homicide victim? When my dog's done with a bone, that's what it looks like, not a spot of blood or meat on it."

The ME told us he'd noticed the bones too, but hadn't found any evidence that an animal had gnawed on them. I asked him if he'd ever seen a stiff with bones that clean.

He shook his head. "Only ones that have been in the ground long enough for the bugs to do their work."

As far as I was concerned, it proved the killer was some new and frightening life form. Nothing else made sense, but before I had a chance to pass that along my cell phone rang. It was Josh calling to ask me if we had an event.

"It sure looks that way."

"Jesus, Ron, you want me to send in reinforcements?"

"Unless I can convince the ME and the local constabulary that we have a problem they can't handle, I'm afraid we'll just end up in a turf war. Not to mention the HAZMAT team would probably cause a panic. Then Dennis would have my job for sure."

I was about to tell him I'd call when I wanted reinforcements, but he said, "Oops, gotta go – our takeout's here" then hung up.

While detective Blanchard and the ME got in a pissing contest over who'd witnessed the most gruesome crime scene, I wandered off to check out the rest of the victim's apartment.

The moment I stepped into his dingy little kitchen, one with an old metal sink cabinet and a hodgepodge of mismatched cupboards, my nose was assaulted by a horrible smell that had a faintly familiar edge I couldn't quite place. A pile of dishes in the sink and a conspicuous buildup of grime around the cupboard door handles suggested that the victim didn't have a live-in girlfriend.

There was barely enough room for a table and two chairs in the little room. The one plate on the table had crusted-over food smudges on it. The chair closest to the plate was further away from the table than the other chair, suggesting that someone had been sitting there and had pushed the chair back to get up.

I tracked the nasty smell to some fuzzy brown mold on one of the dishes piled in the sink, but wasn't able to locate the source of the fainter, disturbingly familiar scent before detective Blanchard burst into the room.

She immediately pinched her nose and made a face. Then she gave the room a quick scan and said, "The way that chair's pushed back, I'd say the perp came up behind our victim, grabbed him around the neck, then dragged him into the other room to cut him open."

I did not buy her theory. "With a wound like that there should be signs of a struggle somewhere. Hell, there should be blood and guts all over the place."

She said, "Maybe the perp took the guy somewhere else to filet him."

I told her the word 'filet' sounded disrespectful.

"How about 'gutted'?" she asked, grinning. "Do you like that better?"

I ignored the crude attempt at humor, but couldn't help noticing how cute her dimples were when she grinned at me, and I wondered what it would be like to kiss her. Then I dismissed the thought and asked her why a drug addled killer would go to the trouble of taking his victim somewhere else to kill him then bring him back.

"I don't know," she said, "maybe it was part of some bizarre cult thing."

I found an out-of-the-way spot of wall to lean on while she looked through the cupboards. I suppose I should have helped her when she got up on her toes to move things on the top shelf, but I was too busy enjoying the view, so much so I almost forgot what I was going to say. "It looks to me as though he was eating something and suddenly felt sick. He went into the other room hoping he'd feel better sitting in the easy chair."

She looked back over her shoulder and frowned at me. "Why are you giving me such a hard time?"

It told her it was "BS."

She grinned, said, "It's 'BS' alright."

I told her 'BS' stood for 'Bio Synthesized', "as in bio-engineered food additives, like the one that ran amok and killed that poor slob out there."

She nodded her head. "Well, judging from this kitchen, you're right about him being a slob."

"And if I'm right about what killed that guy, and it gets the chance to reproduce and spread, it could mean the end for all of us."

Looking at me the way a parent looks at a hopeless child, she shook her head. "Well, that is a dire prediction."

When I told her it was my job to contain outbreaks of this sort, she just shook her head. Then she pulled a chair from the table over to the counter and climbed up on it to feel around over the cupboards. I asked her what she expected to find up there.

"Something a brain damaged killer didn't want us to find."

"Do you really expect to find a weapon that can do that kind of damage hidden up there?"

She spun around and glared at me and said in a voice loud enough to be heard by the uniformed cops out in the hallway. "You can go with your bio-engineered bullshit. But I think there's a rational explanation for this."

I wished I'd met detective Blanchard under better circumstances.

She took a deep breath, and in a quieter, calmer voice, said, "Like maybe the perp didn't want us to know how he killed the guy, so he poured acid on the wound after he killed him."

Then she froze and stared at the wall. I thought maybe she'd come to her senses, when a moment later she snapped her fingers as though she'd had an inspiration. "You think it was an inside job, don't you?"

Then she burst into laughter, fighting it back long enough to say, "This gives a whole new meaning to the term 'eating out.'"

She laughed uncontrollably after that, and when, a few moments later, the ME stepped into the doorway with a scowl on his face, she asked him, "What's eating you?" as she struggled to get her breath back.

The ME shook his head and left the room. Still snickering, she went back to feeling around above the cupboards. Moments later she spun around with an odd look on her face. I asked her what she'd found.

"I can just see tomorrow's headline; 'Consumable Consumes Consumer'. Or how about this: diner becomes dinner or dinner dined on diner?"

Then she climbed down off the counter and came over to me and touched my arm gently. "If you need some company tonight," she said soothingly, "you can come over to my place. I make a killer meatloaf."

I wished I didn't like her. The girl needed help.

She said, "Eat your heart out" then made little snorting noises as she tried to stifle her laughter.

Then she went back to looking through the kitchen

cupboards, and I went back to enjoying the view while I assessed the situation. I wondered why, after bumbling through thirty years of failed relationships, I'd met the girl of my dreams on the same day I found a doomsday event.

Detective Blanchard's attitude wasn't entirely surprising. Besides sounding crazy, the voices of reason and science don't have the appeal of the wildly irresponsible promises made by the food lobby. And the public, always desperate for miracles, believes their hype, despite the protestations of academic naysayers with impeccable credentials. And once the miracle genie's out of his bottle, there's no way to put him back.

That's where my thoughts had wandered off to when the ME appeared at the door and announced he was leaving. Detective Blanchard asked him what was keeping the forensics team.

In the midst of saying, "They had to go out on another call," his cell phone rang.

And while he was talking on his cell phone, Blanchard's cell phone rang. While she was on her call, she stepped over to the sink and pulled a wastebasket out from under it. She dumped the contents on the floor and poked around in the garbage with her foot.

She was still on her call when the ME's call ended. Before he left he said, "Tell detective Blanchard I had to go see another stiff. Apparently it's going to be a busy day; the bodies are piling up."

I wondered if all MEs were as morbid. I supposed it would wear on me too if all of my clients were dead people. Anyway, he had no idea how ominous his comment was, especially considering how the stiff in the other room had died.

Blanchard looked at me when her call ended and she looked genuinely upset. "That was dispatch," she said. "There's been a bunch of grizzly deaths reported in the last couple of hours."

I told her to stop poking at the mess on the floor with her foot, that she was contaminating the crime scene. And as soon as I said it I regretted it, because I didn't want to ruin my chances with her.

She tipped her head slightly to one side. "You don't get it," she said, sounding annoyed. "This was just a drug deal that went bad. It happens all the time. And it doesn't matter how nice we keep the crime scene, we never get the perp."

Having said that forcefully, as if warning me that the topic was closed to discussion, she looked in the victim's refrigerator, saying, "Eureka," immediately after opening the door.

She spun around and looked at me, bright-eyed as a child with a new puppy. "Lookie what I found," she said, holding up a takeout bag from LingLing's.

It explained the familiar smell I couldn't place. I thought about the takeout that would be waiting for me back at the office, and my mouth watered immediately.

Then I remembered the congealed reddish goo on the victim's plate and I realized what it meant. I had a vision of our office staff slumped at their desks with bags of LingLing's takeout in front of them, and all of them disemboweled like the guy in the next room.

I took out my cell phone and hit the speed dial key for Josh. He didn't answer. I tried the office number; the public line never rang more than twice before someone picked up. On the third ring I figured they were probably dead, and so were my chances of getting any kind of backup. By the forth ring I was sure of it. I left a message anyway, just in case, and while I did Blanchard pulled a chicken wing out of the takeout bag. I yelled at her to put it down.

She looked surprised, said to me, "Don't worry; I'll leave you one."

I told her again to put it down as I stood and lunged at her. She took a bite out of it then grinned at me like a fool. I was certain my coworkers had already gone through the agony of having their insides liquefied and eaten. Now I'd be with detective Blanchard while she died the same hideous death.

Grinning at me again, she said, "You're really cute when

you're upset. I think I might even get to like you. As a matter of fact, why don't you come for dinner tonight? My meatloaf's actually quite good."

Didn't matter what I said, so I said nothing, just enjoyed looking at her for our last few minutes.

She gave me a funny look then said, "Really, it's to die for."

ON THE TAKE

Celia got a good look at him when he came through the door just before eleven on a Thursday night, the streetlight outside the bar putting a spotlight on him, as though he was some kind of movie star. This guy was big; probably six feet tall, and heavy but solid-looking, like a football player. And he walked like one of those ex-military guys, as though he was looking for trouble, nothing at all like her husband Jerome who was waiting for them in the apartment next door. She tried to imagine Jerome overpowering this guy but she couldn't do it.

The stranger sat on a stool near the door at the other end of the room. She watched him in the mirror behind the bar so he wouldn't catch her looking. The bartender, one of her husband's no-good acquaintances, was a dark-skinned, little man named Roy, who looked flabby but wasn't fat, looked like he was forty but was only about thirty. When Roy tried to pour the guy's drink from a bottle sitting on the bar, the guy put his hand over his glass and said something she couldn't hear. Then, after a short exchange, the guy tossed a bill on the bar. Roy snatched it up then poured the guy's drink from a bottle he took from the cupboard above the bar where he hid the good stuff.

Roy was always leaning on something, and now he was leaning on the bar talking to the new guy and they were both looking at her. Then the big, good-looking man was coming her way. When Jerome told her they could make some easy cash, she had agreed to do it because money was short again this month, and she didn't want their son Joey sleeping on the street. But now that the guy was on his way over, taking his time and checking her out, she wasn't so sure it was a good idea.

He came and stood next to her holding his drink. She watched him in the mirror while he looked her over, his eyes lingering for a while on her legs then again on her cleavage, studying her as though he was going to buy her, not just rent her.

The ice in her drink had melted, diluting the cheap whiskey, but she held the glass with both hands so he wouldn't see them shaking. Her instincts were telling her to back out before the plan went south and things got dangerous. That's what she was expecting because Jerome always managed to screw things up, but she wanted to know if she was still attractive, wanted to know if this new guy would actually pay a hundred dollars just for a few minutes with her.

He leaned an elbow on the bar, twisting around so he was facing her, then said, "You need a new drink," in a deep, steady voice as he took her glass from her. She looked him over when he turned away and held her glass up to get Roy's attention. He looked even bigger up close. She thought about him lying on her, using her for his pleasure, and wondered what that would feel like. He'd be heavy, and strong enough to do whatever he wanted to her, and the stubble on his cheeks would give her a rash, where it rubbed against her skin. Then she saw he was watching her in the mirror and she looked away to hide her embarrassment.

He held her glass up and told her that cheap whiskey was better served cold, but when Roy came over, he told Roy, "Get her a clean glass and fill it with the stuff I'm having."

As he turned sideways to face her again, and moved a little closer, Celia hoped she was getting a break from the bad lighting because this guy looked younger than her, maybe as young as forty, and in good shape, with a waist as a narrow as hers and shoulders three times that.

Roy winked at her when he brought her drink, putting a key on the counter next to it, and not bothering to hide it. It gave her the creeps the way he always acted like they shared some dirty little secret, and him with that shriveled up skin over his eye where some customer cut him with a broken bottle a few years back. The new guy had been looking at her legs when Roy winked at her. That was good because it was hard enough playing the part without having to explain Roy winking at her.

The guy held a hand out to her. "The name's Vic."

He seemed pretty sure of himself. She liked that in a guy, even if this was business, which meant he didn't have to worry about getting shot down. She put her hand in his, gently, tentatively, barely touching him, dragging her fingertips lightly over his skin as she let go. The thought of those big, rough hands on her thighs stirred up feelings she'd never known with her husband Jerome, an unfamiliar urgent desire that left her feeling edgy and confused, but wanting more.

Vic nodded at her drink. "You got someplace we can go when you finish that?"

He knew she had a place lined up. The key was right there on the bar in front of him. Still, it was nice of the guy to pretend it was his move. She made a show of picking the key up off the bar when she stood up, rising too fast and getting dizzy because she wasn't used to good whiskey.

The guy followed her outside and across the ally to the wooden staircase hanging precariously on the building next door. She had trouble keeping her balance on the stairs because of the booze. It didn't help that the guy was coming up the stairs right behind her, and he could probably see her panties. That was another one of Jerome's bright ideas; "Wear something short," he said. Yeah, easy for him to say; he wasn't going to have some stranger looking up his skirt.

Celia turned on the overhead light as she stepped inside

the apartment, relieved when she finally got the key to work. She was supposed to lead Vic toward the bedroom, past the hall closet where Jerome would be waiting for them, but then Vic came up behind her, putting his hands on her shoulders, kissing her neck. She let her head fall back against his chest. It felt hard, like leaning against a wall. Then his hands were sliding down her arms, across her stomach, along her thighs and up to her breasts; gently at first, like spiders crawling on her skin; his hands getting rougher and more urgent as his breathing came faster and harder, moist and hot on her neck.

Celia broke away because she couldn't stand there while her husband watched Vic feeling her up. She started to walk toward the closet, Vic following close behind her, just the way Roy and Jerome had planned it. Jerome would leap out of the closet behind Vic and subdue him, and even though Vic was a big tough-looking lamb being led to an unlikely slaughter, waiting for it to happen, and leading him into it, made her heart beat so fast and hard she was afraid Vic would hear it.

***

The hall closet was not only much too hot; it was much too small for Jerome who had a serious case of claustrophobia. So by the time Celia showed up, Jerome needed a good, stiff drink.

He'd heard them come up the stairs, had heard their voices, and heard somebody fumbling with the lock. Then a big guy, thick all over like a weight-lifter on steroids, had stepped into the apartment behind his wife. While he watched the guy groping his wife Jerome tried to remember where he'd seen him before.

He'd watched the two of them standing there at the door, the big guy with one hand in her blouse and the other one up her skirt, and Celia licking that big bottom lip of hers while she rubbed against the guy like a cat in heat.

The plan was for her to lead the guy past the closet so Jerome could get behind him, but it looked like the guy was going to take her right there on the kitchen floor, right there where he could watch the whole thing. Celia must've wanted Jerome to see the guy feeling her up. Probably thought she could make him jealous but it didn't work, because watching them was giving him a hard-on.

Then he remembered seeing the guy on the street with that little Italian gangster De Luca, and that was the end of his hard-on, because Jerome had heard some scary things about the guy. No way was he gonna jump this guy, not even with a gun; he wasn't that stupid.

Now here was Celia coming toward him, leading the killer right to him. Jerome leaned back away from the door into the dark. The footsteps stopped right outside the door, one lousy piece of wood between him and a killer. And Celia kept the guy there for what seemed like an eternity, while the sweat beaded up on Jerome's forehead and ran down his face and the closet walls closed in on him. By the time the footsteps receded toward the bedroom, he wanted to scream. It was just like the bitch to do that to him, not to mention picking up a fucking hit man. No wonder he could never get ahead, the way she always worked against him.

A guy like that would probably be rough with her, and it would serve her right, might even teach her a lesson. Then it was quiet for a while; his claustrophobia got worse because he couldn't move for fear he'd make a sound and the guy would find him. Then he heard the bed. It sounded as though the guy was going to drive her right through the floor, and Celia was moaning like she loved it. Bitch never made that much noise at home. He'd have to use the gun on them if he listened to it much longer, so he slipped out of the apartment before the guy got his rocks off.

***

So much for Jerome's plan - she was in the bedroom with a guy who expected her to do things she hadn't expected to do. Thing was, Vic was paying for this with cash, but Jerome would make her pay for it with fresh bruises, and now it was too late to back out. On the up side, it had been a long time since she'd had a good lay.

Celia was still lost somewhere in semi-consciousness, a place she hadn't been to in a long time, when she felt Vic relax; felt his weight settle on her and it felt good, but it meant he was done, so she began to shut down. Later, lying naked on the bed with her eyes closed and the light on, feeling the guy's hands on her skin and knowing he was looking at her, and thinking he must like what he was seeing, she felt good, more like a woman than she'd felt in a very long time. Then she remembered that, once again, Jerome had betrayed her and it left her feeling empty and hurt.

Then Vic was standing by the bed putting on his clothes, the sound of his zipper turning the best thing she'd had in years into something cheap. She wondered if this was how prostitutes felt, and she wished Vic would take her back to wherever it was she'd just been and leave her there.

He took his wallet out, counted out a few bills and put them on the dresser. "I can tell you're new at this. Just so you know; you were worth it."

Celia didn't know what to say to that. She wondered if it was a compliment as she watched Vic put on his tie and check it in the mirror over the dresser.

Then he turned around to face her. "Maybe we could have a different arrangement. There'd still be money in it for you, but it wouldn't have to feel like it was just business."

He came over to the bed and put a pen and a business card on the mattress next to her. "Write your name and phone number on here if you're interested."

Most of what had happened wasn't supposed to happen, and she certainly hadn't expected an offer like that. She thought maybe she could fall for this guy, and even though Jerome would kill her if he caught her having an affair, it would almost be worth it.

Vic was standing next to the bed, looking at her lying there naked. "If you're worried about somebody finding out, I'll take care of it; doesn't matter who he is."

She was tempted to do it, until she thought about Jerome answering the phone, about this guy asking for her, and how that would play out. Jerome had beaten her for a lot less before. So, what she really wanted to do was go home.

After Vic left, she checked the hall closet to be sure Jerome wasn't in there. She half expected to find him passed out on the floor in a drunken stupor. It would've explained why things went wrong, but it didn't really matter, because whatever had gone wrong, Jerome would blame her for it, and he'd use it as an excuse to beat her.

She thought about Vic and the sex while she got dressed. On the up side, she had something she would remember for the rest of her life. It wasn't perfect, but it was better than the sex ever was with Jerome, better than anything that had happened to her in a long time. On the down side, no matter how much she wanted to see Vic again, she would never have anything but the memory of this night with him.

It was a long walk through a bad neighborhood to the cheap apartment they rented in a housing project where drugs and crime were as predictable as the passage of time. And Jerome was waiting for her when she got home, standing there with his hand out like a beggar, telling her she'd better hand over the money.

Wanting to hurt him, but knowing it wasn't going to happen, she blurted out, "Where the fuck were you, asshole?"

Jerome started to pace around the kitchen acting like he was on something. "Never mind where I was. A hundred dollars; that was the deal, even if you're not worth it. Now unless you want me to hurt you, hand it over."

"You didn't do a god-damned thing to earn it and neither did that puss-bag Roy."

"Yeah, well that wasn't complaining I heard coming from the bedroom."

Not many things could put Celia in a rage, but that did it. "You fucking pervert. You were listening."

"What was I supposed to do?"

"You had a gun."

"The guy's an assassin, for Christ's sake."

"You'll take care of him. That's what you said when you made me play your stupid game."

"Yeah, but the size of that guy?"

"I know how big he was, you asshole. He was on top of me, remember."

Jerome pointed a finger at her. "Next time, be more careful who you hook up with."

She couldn't decide whether to scream or look for a sharp knife, so she grabbed a saucepan, the only thing within reach, and threw it at him as hard as she could, yelling, "Roy picked him out, not me. And tell me you didn't say 'next time'."

Jerome ducked it easily, the pan bouncing off the wall with a new dent. Then he glared at her. "You wanna know what I think? I think you wanted to screw him, 'cause you could've walked away when you were still at the bar, but you didn't."

Making him mad would have its price, but she couldn't help herself. If she didn't let it out she'd lose her mind. "You failed at everything you ever did, and I can live with that; God knows I have, but I'm never gonna forgive you for what you did tonight, you coward."

Celia had hardly gotten the words out before he was across the room. She didn't have time to block the punch, but she did turn her head so she wouldn't get a black eye this time.

As she rubbed the spot where his punch had landed, she said, "That excites you, doesn't it?"

Before he stormed out, he said, "Word gets out on the street about you and that guy, you're gonna be one sorry fucking whore."

Celia knew it was just a matter of time before Jerome beat her for it, because Roy would tell somebody about it. She knew he would. She was just glad their son Joey hadn't been home to hear what Jerome said about her.

***

It was after midnight when Joey got home. He went straight to the bathroom to clean up because he didn't want his mother to see the blood, but she was in there cleaning the sink when he opened the door. He knew he looked bad, but his mother gasped when she saw him, so he looked in the mirror. He looked like he'd been breaking rocks with his face. Next thing he knew his mother was holding his chin with one hand and wetting a washcloth with the other.

As he pushed her hand away, she said, "Poor baby, who did this to you?"

He touched the blossoming bruise on her cheek. "Who did that?"

She pushed Joey's hand away. "Don't get smart with me."

He yelled, "Get out, just get out," because he couldn't think of anything else. She could do that to him; make him so mad his mind went blank.

On her way out she told him she was going to get him some ice for the swelling. He locked the door after she left. Then he took a good look at the mess on his shoulders. It was gonna hurt, and knowing he'd see those same kids the next day at school wouldn't make it any easier. When he took a leak, he watched his urine turn the toilet water pink, thinking he would've ended up in the hospital again if some stranger hadn't stopped those kids, and thinking what he needed was a gun.

A soft rap on the door was followed by, "I brought you an ice pack. I'll leave it here on the floor."

He told her to go away as he dabbed at the dried blood with a washcloth. And every time he winced, he imagined how different things would've been if he'd had a gun. He took his shirt off to check for bruises. Some were already beginning to show as dark patches on the porcelain white skin stretched tightly over his boney skeleton.

Growing up, he'd always assumed he'd put some meat over his bones, but it never happened. The skinny, acne-riddled, kid looking back at him from the mirror, the one with a big nose and unruly hair, also had a slight case of palsy. It was enough to make his movements look jerky and awkward, which made him a laughing stock at school. A gun would stop it.

***

On Friday evening, Harvey Manheim was pacing the floor of his kitchen, in his apartment upstairs over the jewelry store that had been in his family for three generations. He didn't remember ever being so sick, not in all of his eighty-three years. He didn't remember a lot of things these days, but he was sure he'd never been so sick he couldn't walk straight.

Manheim muttered to himself as he paced, "Sure, when I need a loan the fucking banks dry up like an old woman's tit, so I gotta borrow fifty thousand from that crook Julian before I run out of stock. Then it's "Bend over Harvey', life's got another surprise for you; business is gonna drop like a dead bird, so you're gonna have to scrape together ten thousand a month just to cover the interest."

He threw a glass against the wall, but it didn't help; so he threw another one. That didn't help either so he started muttering again. "Had to fucking get sick too, didn't ya Harvey? And now who's gonna deliver this month's payment?"

And then he remembered his niece Celia. She had a boy. He didn't remember the kid being too bright, but Harvey didn't need someone with brains, so he gave her a call.

She sounded upset when she answered the phone, but he was way too sick to care about anybody else's problems. "This is your uncle Harvey."

"God, you sound like shit."

He never did like Celia, and couldn't imagine what Jerome saw in her. "I got a job for your kid."

"His name is Joey, Harv."

"Yeah, great, I'm happy for him."

He didn't hear anything after that so he figured he had pissed her off; touchy God-damned broad. "Hey, you still there?"

"What kind of job?"

"The kind that pays him forty bucks, and all he's gotta do is deliver something. You think he can handle that?"

"Why not do it yourself?"

"'Cause I'm too sick to leave the house. I sound like shit, remember? But he's gotta do it tonight."

"I don't want my Joey getting mixed up in anything illegal."

What he wanted to say was, "The only way a dumb kid like Joey is ever gonna make any money is doing something illegal," but he needed the kid, so he pretended he didn't hear her and hung up. He'd break the bad news to her about Joey some other time.

***

Celia knocked on Joey's door then counted to ten before opening it, because there are some things a mother doesn't want to walk in on. Joey was sitting at his desk so his back was to the door. He had a book open but he wasn't fooling anyone; he hadn't read a book in years.

Celia stood in the doorway. "You remember my Uncle Harvey?"

Joey turned around in his chair. "What about him?'

It hurt her heart to see the bruises. She wished she could sit him on her lap and hold him the way she had when he was little. "He's gonna give you forty dollars just to run an errand for him."

She expected him to jump at the chance to make some easy money, but what she got was, "I don't feel like it."

"Where else are you gonna get that kind of money, Joey?"

"Go away."

"If you're gonna do it, you have to do it right now."

She asked him to be careful as he walked past her muttering obscenities, because she didn't want her boy coming back bloody again.

***

Roy gave a nod to Julian when Julian and his friends came into the bar, a sign of respect he resented having to make. Julian didn't do anything for him when that customer cut his face up, and Roy still held a grudge about it. He figured Julian owed him something for it, but all he got from Julian was a reprimand. Julian even had the nerve to tell him he'd been careless, and when Roy argued with him about it, Julian told him he didn't have to pay Roy's hospital bills.

Julian and his friends sat in one of the booths by the front windows, the one farthest away from the bar, and Roy knew they sat there so he couldn't hear what they were saying. Long past middle age and frail, the four throwbacks seemed unaware that they no longer ruled the streets; that their empires were crumbling as fast as their bodies were decaying. Although Julian was the oldest and feeblest of the four has-beens, having grown pudgy and weak from too many easy years, the other three deferred to him because of the reputation he'd earned before most of the people in the neighborhood were born.

Julian and his friends came every Thursday night for drinks and stayed till closing, dressed in outdated suits downing his best Scotch like parched desert travelers drinking water at an oasis. It was some kind of ritual, eating the same thing, at the same time, on the same day, every week. So, every Thursday night, Roy put a reserved sign on the table in the booth where Julian liked to sit.

Roy got the idea for hiding a microphone under their table from a television show. First he convinced Julian to spring for the money to replace the worn out carpet. Then he ran the wire for the microphone beneath the carpet underlayment while the workers were on break. Now whenever Julian and his friends came in, Roy put on his headphones and listened to them while he pretended to listen to his Walkman.

That particular night the talk started with Roberto, a short pudgy man sitting across from Julian who always managed to get red sauce on his shirt. "The star receiver on the local, big-ten football team was into me for a lot of money, a lot more than he could cover. So I sent him on an errand with my boy Sergey."

Julian interrupted Roberto when he said the name 'Sergey'. "What the hell kind of name is that?"

"What difference does it make?"

"Sounds like another fucking Slav."

Roberto ignored Julian's outburst. "So, like I was saying, Sergey makes the kid break some guy's kneecap with a bat."

"Yeah, and how'd that work out?"

"Made the kid puke, but it made him real cooperative too."

The has-been sitting next to Julian, the one wearing an expensive suit from an era most people were too young to remember, said, "So what?"

"So he's gonna throw the home-coming game tonight to cover his debt. Odds are running ten-to-one in their favor. I thought you might want in on the action."

Julian got so loud that Roy could hear him without the earphones. "That means I'm gonna have to cover the bets against them at ten-to-one."

"Hey, anyone dumb enough to bet against a ten-to-one favorite probably doesn't have a lot of money."

"Are you kidding? The rich fucking alumni always bet their team no matter what the odds. Losing a few thousand is nothing to them."

"So call Vegas and put enough down to cover your losses and make a little extra. That's what I'm gonna do."

Roy didn't smile very often, but he was smiling when he called Jerome's cell phone. He always bet small, and he always had Jerome place the bet so De Luca wouldn't suspect that he had overheard the old farts talking. It wouldn't make up for the scar, but if he put it all together, even after splitting the take with Jerome, he'd raked in some serious green since he put the microphone in.

***

Even if he got the whole forty bucks, Joey still wouldn't have enough to buy a gun, so he was angry when he pounded on his great uncle's door and yelled, "It's me, Joey. Open up."

From inside he heard, "Yeah, yeah, I'm comin', hold your water."

Manheim answered his door in a bathrobe, looking startled, as though he didn't recognize Joey at first. Then his lips turned up to form a grin as he let out an audible chuckle. "Looks like somebody beat the shit outta you?"

Joey was tempted to kick the old guy where it would do the most good, but instead he reached for the briefcase Manheim was holding. "That what you want delivered?"

The old guy held it back out of Joey's reach. "You know who Julian De Luca is?"

"Yeah, everybody knows that."

"Then make sure he gets this."

The old man handed him the briefcase. "And don't do anything stupid like opening it, understand?"

Opening the briefcase hadn't occurred to Joey, not until Manheim told him he shouldn't do it. And Joey only half heard the old guy say, "That could get you killed," because he was looking at the case, wondering how much cash was in it.

Then Manheim said, "Hey, what's the matter with you," so loud it startled Joey. The old guy was holding an envelope out. "You want the forty bucks, don't ya?"

Joey grabbed the envelope, stuffed it into a coat pocket, and got out of there in a hurry. He was on his way down the stairs when Manheim opened his door and yelled after him, "If Julian doesn't get that today he's gonna send somebody after it."

Joey turned down the first deserted alley he came to; walking far enough in to get behind a dumpster so people on the sidewalk wouldn't be able to see him. He tried the latch on the briefcase. It was locked, which meant there had to be something valuable in it. He tried beating the briefcase with a brick he found in the alley. The exertion drained some of the anger and frustration he'd felt since he was beaten, but the briefcase was still intact in spite of the effort. When he got his breath back, he swung the flat side of the briefcase against a corner of the dumpster, using two hands and putting his weight into it.

When it broke, bills floated to the ground like autumn leaves. He picked up a wad of them, checking the denominations, feeling a rush when he saw that it was mostly tens and twenties. It was enough money for a gun and a whole lot more. Then he sat on the pavement, breathing hard and studying his handiwork. It was a lot of money, so much money nobody was going to miss a few hundred dollars, but the briefcase was destroyed. He couldn't take it to Julian looking like that, so he took the rest of the money out, filling his pockets with it and threw the case in the dumpster. On his way home he felt better than he had in a long time.

His mother came to the door to meet him when he got there. "Well?"

"His place smelled like old people. I wanted to throw up."

She held her hand out. "Where's the money"

Joey started to panic, was backing away from her when he remembered the envelope and realized that it was the forty dollars she wanted. He gave it to her, relieved that she didn't know about the real money, but she looked at him funny and he knew the look, knew she was suspicious of something.

She said, "I'll hold this for you so you're not tempted to buy something you shouldn't," but she still had that look on her face, as though he'd done something wrong.

On his way to his room he realized he should've taken his twenty dollars out of the envelope. To cover his mistake he yelled, "I knew you were gonna take it all. That's why I didn't want do it."

Safely in his room, he stuffed the money into his school backpack and put it under the pile of dirty clothes on the floor to discourage his mother from picking it up. Then he lay back on his sagging mattress and looked at the familiar stains on the ceiling. He knew that much cash had to be for something illegal, probably gambling or drugs. Who'd have thought Uncle Harvey was connected? It was pretty funny until he really thought about it. Then he sat up with a start and looked at the pile of clothes covering the backpack that was full of cash, cash that belonged to the mob. His great uncle knew he had the money, and the old fart didn't like him, never had, and that's when Joey realized he was in a lot of trouble.

He flopped back on his bed to think of a way out of the mess he'd made. He grabbed a basketball off the floor by the bed, absently tossing it at a ceiling stain. A couple of tosses later he'd worked up a sweat, not from tossing the ball but from worrying about the money. The next toss knocked a piece of sagging plaster loose. Sitting up with a start and brushing the plaster dust off, he said, "Shit," because his dad would probably beat him for it.

And that's when the answer came to him. It seemed to come out of nowhere, and it was so good, for one brief moment he actually wondered if it was one of those divine revelations his mother talked about. But he had no time for her nonsense; he had things to do.

He got an old shoebox out of his closet and emptied it, stuffing most of the cash from his backpack into it. Then he opened his door a crack and listened until he heard his mother doing something in the kitchen before sneaking into his parents' room, where he put the box in the top drawer of his father's dresser. He didn't close the drawer all the way because he wanted his father to notice and find the box. Then he snuck back to his own room.

For the first time in his seventeen years he was going to be driving the train, and it was an express train to success, and it was his idea; not bad for a kid. He snuck out of the apartment so he wouldn't have to lie to his mother about where he was going.

***

Celia knew Joey was up to something. A mother can tell. At seventeen Joey was old enough, and the neighborhood was bad enough, that he could get mixed up with some dangerous people. It's what most of the young men from the project did. And there wasn't any point in confronting him, because whatever it was, he'd lie about it. So Celia got out the cheap whiskey and poured herself a glass of serenity then sat at the table looking for answers in it.

By the time she was halfway through the glass, the alcohol had taken her back to a bar where a good-looking guy was buying her expensive bourbon. Warm and pleasantly fuzzy by the time the whiskey was gone, she went to her room to lie down and fantasize about a big, good-looking guy named Vic doing all sorts of things to her, unable to control his desire.

She saw the open drawer in Jerome's dresser as soon as she stepped into the room. Curiosity drew her to the cardboard box that hadn't been there the day before. She couldn't see it and not open it, but she opened it reluctantly because she expected to find proof of Jerome's continuing infidelity in it. Jerome liked to collect trophies.

She took the box out of the drawer and opened it, and when she saw the money, she asked herself, "What the fuck did you do, Jerome," saying it out loud as she sat down on the bed, using a hand to steady herself. She stared silently at the box on her lap until the thought of Jerome coming home and finding her with it frightened her. Then she began counting the money. She didn't count all of it; just enough to know it wasn't petty cash.

The stupid son-of-a-bitch was mixed up in drugs or one of the other forms madness took in their neighborhood. Maybe she should've seen it coming. Maybe not seeing it made her a failure as a wife, but the real failure was Jerome as a dad. He was putting them all in danger. The dumb son-of-a-bitch probably had Joey mixed up in it. It would explain why Joey had been acting strange.

Then another disturbing thought hit her, leaving a

bruise on her self-esteem that would take longer to heal than any bruise Jerome put on her face. Why'd he make her play the whore if he had all this money? And, as if that wasn't bad enough, Jerome had told her that the scam was Roy's idea; so maybe Roy had been there with him while Vic had his way with her. She should have stopped herself there, but her mind conjured up an image of Jerome and Roy watching her having sex with Vic, a thought so repulsive shaking her head didn't dislodge it.

When she'd recovered her wits, she counted out a thousand dollars. Not enough for Jerome to notice unless he counted it. When she heard a key in the deadbolt on the front door, she became frantic, putting the box back in the drawer, fumbling with it, trying to make it look the way it was when she found it. She was on her way to the kitchen when Jerome came in.

***

As soon as Jerome stepped into the apartment, he knew Celia was up to something. He was sure of it because when she walked past him she didn't hit him with any of her usual angry comments, but he didn't have time for her nonsense. He went straight to his room to change before going out for the night, and he noticed the open drawer immediately. It didn't matter how many times he beat her for messing with his things, she never seemed to learn. He leaned on the dresser, breathing deeply, trying to get his anger under control. He was about to go looking for her when he spotted the box that didn't belong there.

There was more cash in the box than he'd seen in a long time, maybe ever. But any concerns about where it came from would have to wait because Roy had given him a hot tip, and now he could turn it into some serious money.

Without bothering to count it, he made a large roll out of the bills. He'd let the flunky at the bookie's window count it because that's what they were good at, and if he didn't hurry he wouldn't have time to place the bet.

On his way out he spotted Celia sitting at the kitchen table holding an empty glass. He yelled to her from the hallway. "Tonight's the night I get what's coming to me." When she didn't answer him he went over and kicked the leg of her chair.

He put his hand on the back of her neck as he bent over, whispering in her ear, "You're gonna be real sorry if I find out you earned this by whoring around on me."

Celia's voice sounded as flat and dead as old road kill. "What the hell are you talking about?"

He tightened his grip on her neck. "When I get back, I'm gonna teach you a lesson you'll never forget."

***

Julian was annoyed when Roy came over to their table to tell him that one of his clerks was on the phone. He went and sat at the bar while the clerk told him that Manheim hadn't showed up with his payment. Julian dialed Vic's cellphone number. After six rings he got Vicks' voicemail.

After the beep he said, "Where the hell are you? I gotta a job I want done tonight."

As he was hanging up the phone, he said to Roy, who was leaning on the bar watching him, "Ungrateful Slav doesn't answer his phone. I ought to punch his fucking ticket."

Roy held a glass up to the light to check it after wiping it with a bar rag. "Hard to find good help these days, ain't it?"

When Julian thought about how things had been going down the toilet lately, it made him weary. "Fucking guy doesn't know how lucky he is to be working for me. If the local kids weren't such chicken-shits, I would've hired one of them instead."

Roy gave him a nod, "Like I said; it's hard to find good help."

Julian glared at him. "I am gonna pull the plug on that no-good, Eastern-European, half-breed one of these days, and if you're not careful you'll be next, asshole."

Then the phone rang and it was Vic asking him what

he wanted. What he wanted was to kick the shit out of the arrogant prick who just asked him what he wanted, but he had bigger fish to fry. "I loaned an old friend, a guy named Harvey Manheim, fifty big ones. He's been paying me ten grand a month real regular like, but he didn't show today."

Vic asked, "What do you want me to do about him?"

"Jesus, you can't figure that out for yourself?"

Julian pictured Vic looking back at him with that stupid, blank stare of his. "Manheim probably thinks I'll let him off the hook for it because he's an old friend. You do whatever you gotta do so it doesn't ever happen again, because that's how it starts. Word gets around and next thing you know somebody else is late. So everybody makes their payments on time, doesn't matter who they are."

Back at the table with his friends, Julian made a grand sweeping gesture with his drink that ended with him holding it up over the table. "Here's to the old days when the only people who fucked us were our prostitutes."

***

The security chain on the apartment door went tight, giving Vic a two inch wide view of a frail looking old man in a bathrobe. "Mr. Manheim?"

"Yeah, who the hell are you?"

"Julian De Luca sent me."

The door closed then opened. Vic leaned away from the sick looking old man as he stepped past him into the apartment. Once inside, he backed away across a cluttered, dingy room reeking of stale air and the pungent-smelling ointments old men use. Vic sat on the couch and studied the frail little man who was not much over five feet tall, with a nose and mustache that reminded Vic of a rodent. Manheim was stooped over, moving slowly, probably a victim of arthritis, which would explain the gnarled fingers. A few strands of thin white hair stood off his head like wisps of smoke.

The old guy sounded as though he was drowning in

phlegm. "Tell me what you want, and be quick about it 'cause I don't feel so good."

"Julian says it doesn't matter if you're a friend or not; you gotta make your payments just like everybody else."

Manheim frowned at him. "You're too late."

Julian didn't pay Vic to listen to excuses. "What's that mean?"

"It means I already sent it to him."

Maybe he did, or maybe the old guy was stalling for time. Either way, Vic had come there expecting to beat the shit out of Manheim: that's what Julian paid him to do. He just had to figure out how to hurt the old man without crippling him so badly he couldn't make his payments, because old guys didn't heal so well.

Vic got up and crossed the room toward Manheim. The old guy bumped into an end table as he was backing away, and some of the stuff on the table fell to the floor, including a framed picture of a guy in a dress uniform, a soldier who looked a lot like a young version of Manheim. The soldier was getting a medal, and there was a medal in a little plastic case on the floor next to the picture.

Vic picked up the medal, holding it up close to study it. "What was this for?"

"I took out a machine gun nest; did it single-handed; ran right at the son-of-a-bitch like I was invincible."

Manheim rambled on about his heroics, but Vic knew the old guy wasn't telling it the way it really happened, because if he was, he'd stumble through it as he tried to remember what had happened and thought about how to tell it. This story sounded like it had been told too many times and polished a little more with each telling, some of the truth getting lost with each polishing.

Vic was thinking about how pathetic the old guy was, thinking it was reason enough for Vic to live large and die at the top of his game, when the old guy came at him, no weapon, just his fists.

Vic admired the old guy for having the balls to attack him; didn't matter if it was like getting hit by a girl, it was still a gutsy thing to do. Under different circumstances he might've learned to like the old guy, but business is business, so he hit Manheim in the stomach; his fist sinking into the old guy's stomach like raw bread dough. Then Vic stepped back so he'd be out of harm's way if the old guy retched, but all the guy did was collapse on the couch.

Vic waited while Manheim struggled to get his breath back. When he finally did, the old guy said, "I hired a kid to take the money to Julian."

Vic went over and grabbed one of Manheim's feet and pulled him off the couch. He felt something give when his shoe connected with the old guy's face.

Then he knelt down close to Manheim who seemed to have left the planet. "You can tell me where the money is, or we can do this all over again, and it'll be worse next time."

It was difficult for Vic to make out what the old guy was saying through the mucus and the blood. "A kid named Joey Libertore was supposed to deliver it for me."

Vic got the kid's address from Manheim then sat down in a chair to study him, trying to decide if he was telling the truth after all. And he decided that maybe he was, which presented an opportunity. Some snotty kid had ten thousand dollars, and that was a lot of opportunity. And a couple of thousand would almost make up for Julian calling him an ungrateful fucking Slav when he'd called earlier. Vic was still pissed off about that.

The old guy was watching him, probably wondering what Vic was going to do to him next. Thing was, Vic didn't know yet either, so he sat there watching Manheim for a while. Vic had never been the first horse out of the gate, but he got the answer eventually, and when he did, he talked through it because thinking out loud was easier. "So you hired some kid to deliver the money for you."

Manheim nodded, as though Vic was finally getting it, but Vic didn't care about Manheim any more. "So the kid comes here to pick up the money, and he sees how much there is, and he wonders what an old fart like you needs all that money for. And the kid starts thinking, if you spent it on a hooker, you'd probably die before you got her done, so why not be a Good Samaritan and save her from killing you, right?"

Then it occurred to Vic that the old guy might tell someone else about hiring the kid. If word got to DeLuca that the kid was supposed to deliver the payment, Vic would lose his chance at the money. DeLuca might even come after him for it.

Vic took his gun out and walked over and held it in Manheim's face. He gave the old man a minute or so to think about dying then shot him. Manheim was already dead when Vic told him he wasn't invincible, that, "It was just dumb luck that machine gun didn't kill you sixty years ago."

Before he left Manheim's place Vic wiped his prints off of Manheim's shoe and the doorknob. Now all he had to do was find the kid. He'd keep a couple of thousand dollars for himself. The kid's parents would be so afraid of Julian finding out, they'd make up the missing cash. And if he could get the kid alone, he'd let him handle the gun then plant it at Manheim's place to frame the kid for the murder.

***

Joey found out Julian was at Roy's place by asking around on the street. When the guy behind the bar told him, "No kids allowed," Joey lied to him, told him Julian had sent for him. He spotted Julian and went and stood by their table.

When Julian saw him he said, "No kids allowed."

"I gotta talk to you, Mr. De Luca."

"What about?"

"Harvey Manheim."

"What about him?"

"He asked me to bring you a briefcase."

"Yeah, then where is it?"

"My dad took it. I told him it was for you, but he took it anyway."

Julian grabbed Joey's shirt and pulled him over to the table. "You wouldn't lie to me, would ya, kid?"

Joey shook his head and tried not to wet himself, thinking maybe his plan wasn't so great after all.

"Something bad's gonna happen to you if I find out you lied to me."

Julian and the other three men at the table were all staring at him. He felt the urge to say something, anything to break the tension, but he was afraid he'd say something stupid.

When Julian let go of his shirt he felt the relief all the way down to his bladder.

What's your name, kid?"

"Joey Libertore."

"Yeah, and where do you live?"

All he'd thought about since he had the idea to frame his Dad was getting a gun and having some money, but now, saying his address out loud to Julian, he felt scared, right down to the cold, goose-bumpy skin on his arms. "In the project on Lincoln Avenue near Twelfth Street, Building F, Apartment 64."

As Julian scribbled the address on a napkin he told Joey, "You done good, kid. Now get out of here."

Joey couldn't get out fast enough, but once outside he knew exactly where he was going; because he had enough money in his coat pocket for a small arsenal. He put his hood up over his head so no one would recognize him and went to find the guy who sold thirty-eight caliber courage.

Later, on his way home, after stopping to load the handgun, he felt safe for the first time in years. His thoughts drifted back to De Luca's money. He pictured his dad finding it, and he pictured De Luca's thugs finding his dad. They wouldn't believe his dad, would probably beat him, and might even kill him. Joey had thought about killing his dad, had actually thought about it more than once. This way he'd miss out on the satisfaction of doing it himself, but this way was a lot safer.

Then he thought about the kids who'd beaten him and

he smiled. He'd make them pay big time when he caught up with them.

***

Vic made sure the hallway was empty before he knocked on the door of Apartment 64 in building F, because if things got messy, he didn't want somebody around who could ID him later. He knocked and waited.

He hadn't heard from Celia so he hadn't expected to see her again, certainly not answering the door to Apartment 64 of building F. The two of them stood there looking at each other with the door open, Celia looking as though she'd seen a ghost. Vic heard a door close behind him and realized he was still standing in the hallway where he could be seen. It was a mistake and, like Julian always said, they couldn't afford mistakes in their business.

Celia held the door open for him, but looked away when walked in past her, as though she had a secret. He figured it was about the money, figured she probably knew her husband had it. Celia closed the door behind him.

She frowned when he asked her if she had a kid named Joey. The frown made her look older, got Vic wondering how old Celia really was, because makeup can take the years off, and so can being horny. And the night they hooked up, she was wearing makeup and he was horny. But old or not, there was something about her, about the way she looked that conjured up an image of her lying naked on a bed, with her eyes closed and her lips parted, inviting him to take her.

She asked him what he wanted Joey for. It wasn't easy for him to shake the image of her. "You know who Julian De Luca is?"

She asked him again why he was looking for Joey, but Vic had seen her flinch when he said Julian's name, so he knew she was guilty of something. "Joey's dad has some money that belongs to Julian."

She thought about the cash in the drawer, and how stupid Leroy had to be to steal from a mobster. "Why are you

69

asking about Joey if his dad has the money?"

"If you help me get Julian's money back, nothing bad will happen to the kid."

"His dad's not here."

"Well, what's his name and where can I find him?"

"It's Jerome, and he's probably at that topless bar over on Madison near Fifth."

Vic gave Celia a business card like the one he tried to get her to write her phone number on the night they met. "That's my cellphone number. Call me when he comes back."

For a few uncomfortable moments Vic tried to find the words to talk her into some kind of arrangement, one that included getting into her panties on a regular basis. He soon gave up because he wasn't good with words, but before he left, he told Celia, "You gotta help me out here, 'cause you and the kid won't be safe until Julian gets his money."

***

Jerome got home just before ten, and went right to the living room to turn on the television. The football game was almost over. The local kids, the ones who were favored ten-to-one, were behind with only seven seconds left on the clock. They were close enough to kick a field goal but they needed four points to win, so they needed a touchdown. The next play would be a pass to their star receiver. If he missed it, Jerome would be a rich man.

Jerome watched wonder boy sprint away from his man-to-man coverage and cut across the end zone all by himself. The quarterback drilled a bullet into the far corner of the end zone, wonder boy diving for it, a heroic, arm's-length effort with great hang time.

The kid got his hands on the ball but dropped it when he tried to pull it in. It seemed like they showed the instant replay a hundred times, the sportscasters saying it looked like he dropped the ball on purpose, and droning on about the same kid fumbling another catch earlier in the game. Jerome laughed because that kid's troubles were just beginning, but his were finally over.

Neither Celia nor Joey had been around to see his big win, and wasn't that just like them? The kid was never home anyway, but Celia would do something like that just for spite. "You out there, bitch? Hey, I'm talking to you."

After a while she appeared at the door with her hands on her hips as though she was mad, but it didn't bother him because she was always mad lately. He held the claim ticket up for her to see. "I just turned that little wad of cash you put in my drawer into some serious money. What do ya think of that?"

Celia had a blank look on her face, like she couldn't put a thought together even if he gave her all the pieces. He shook the ticket at her. "That's ten-to-one, you dumb bitch."

***

Celia followed Jerome into the hallway, watched him put the claim ticket in his coat pocket. She thought about the thousands he'd left with, thought about what ten times that much would look like.

She pulled on his sleeve while he was putting on his coat so he couldn't get his arm in it. "What's your hurry, big guy?"

Then she pointed at the living room. "I've got something for you."

"Yeah, what makes you think I want it?"

"Oh, you want this." She rubbed his groin and nodded toward the living room. "Go on in there and get comfortable. I'm gonna get you a drink and then I'm gonna do things to you that you'll never forget."

Jerome hung his coat back on the hook. "It's about fucking time."

When she started toward Joey's room, he asked her what she was doing.

"If I give him some money he'll go out."

"Maybe he oughta stay and get an education."

She put her index finger in her mouth, pulling it out slowly, letting it linger on her lower lip as she said, "You don't want me holding back. I know you don't."

Jerome headed for the living room mumbling something about her being sorry if she was wasting his time.

Celia went to Joey's room and walked in without knocking. Joey, who was sitting on his bed, pulled a blanket over his lap as he said, "What the hell?"

He leaned away from her when she moved in close enough to whisper, "Your dad just won a lot of money."

Joey started to say something but she cut him off. "Shut up and listen. The claim ticket is in his coat pocket. Go cash it in and bring the money back here while I keep him busy."

Then she tossed Vic's card on Joey's lap. "On your way back, stop somewhere and call this guy. Tell him your dad's here and he's got the money. When you get back, count out ten thousand dollars and put it in your dad's coat pocket. You got all that?"

"Yeah, yeah, I got it, now get out."

"Come on, Joey, you gotta hurry. I don't know how long I can keep your father here. Jesus, if you knew what I gotta do to keep him here . . ."

"Why do you do shit like that?"

"I'd do a lot worse than that to get us out of this place."

"Well, I'm gonna fix it so he can't hurt us anymore."

"I don't want to hear any more talk like that, you understand?"

Joey pointed at her bruise. "He wouldn't dare do that if I had a gun."

"And I told you, I don't like that kind of talk. Now get going."

She'd have a talk with him about guns, try to get the notion out of his head before he started down a road leading to a judge's bench, but that would have to wait. She hurried back to Jerome before he changed his mind and left.

Celia heard the door when Joey got back home half an hour later. She heard him go into the kitchen. It took her mind off what she was doing to Jerome, even though she'd thought about doing the same thing to Vic, but that was different. Her knees screamed at her when she got up. They'd be sore and stiff in the morning, a reminder of what she'd done, but she could live with bruises on her knees. She hiked her skirt up so she could sit on Jerome's lap, knowing he wouldn't be able to get it up again.

Jerome pushed her away. "I'd really like to stay for more, but I gotta cash that ticket in before the place closes."

He walked out of the room and down the hall toward the bathroom. When she heard the door close, she went to the kitchen. Joey was sitting at the table with a roll of cash in front of him. Celia went over and leaned on the table next to him. When Joey started to say something, she held her finger up to silence him, whispering, "Did you put the ten thousand in his pocket?"

"Just like you told me."

"And you called Vic?"

"Just like you told me."

Celia noticed something was holding Joey's jacket out in the back. When he caught her looking back there, she reached in fast and pulled the gun out before he could stop her.

He was trying to stand up, saying, "Hey, that's mine," but she pushed him back down in the chair and told him to stay there.

The gun frightened her; it didn't matter that Joey got it to protect her from Jerome. It was proof she needed to get her boy out of the tenements before he gave in to the madness around them, no matter what it took. She heard the toilet flush, heard the water running and knew it was Jerome combing his hair, not washing his hands.

She went to the closet to put the gun in Jerome's coat pocket. She didn't care what Jerome did with it as long as Joey didn't have it. That's where Jerome caught up with her. "What the hell you doin' with my coat?"

She rubbed a hand on his crotch and was relieved she didn't feel a reaction in his pants.

He shoved her so hard she bounced against the wall. "Need more of that, do ya? You just wait till I get back."

She watched him go into the living room and drain his glass of whiskey, and she knew the only way she could keep him there was to make him angry. But it would be easier to take the beating this time, knowing it would be the last one. She stood in front of the apartment door.

When Jerome saw her there he took a deep breath and told her to get out of the way but Celia shook her head and stood her ground.

Jerome said, "I don't have time for this," but didn't show any signs he was about to lose his temper, so she said, "You're not half the man Vic is."

When he made a fist she knew he wasn't leaving anytime soon.

***

Standing in the hallway outside apartment 64 holding his gun in his right hand, Vic was about to knock on the door when he heard a commotion inside that sounded like somebody getting pushed around. But when he pounded on the door, the noise coming from inside stopped. He checked the hall to be sure none of the neighbors had come out to see about the noise. Then a teenage kid opened the door to apartment 64, probably the one who'd called him, and from somewhere inside, he heard an angry voice ask who was at the door.

The kid said, "Some guy I've never seen."

The same angry voice was closer to the door this time. "What are ya, stupid? Close the God-damned door."

The door started to close. The kid stepped back. He looked frightened of something. Vic grabbed the edge of door with his left hand then put his weight behind it, slamming it back, hard. It connected with something. He stepped inside, closing the door behind him. A middle-aged man dressed like he was on vacation in Hawaii lunged at Vic. Vic hit him with the flat of his gun, knocking him to the floor.

The guy held his hands to his head. He was having trouble sitting up. "Who the fuck are you?"

The kid had gone somewhere and Celia had come out of the kitchen. The light was coming from above her and to her left, leaving most of her face in shadow but outlining it, highlighting her full lips, and tracing the line of her dress as it fell over her breasts and down past her hips. Vic had decided on the way over she wasn't worth the risk; that there were plenty of good-looking women around, but now that she was right there, and looking better than he remembered, he wasn't so sure.

He touched the bruise on her cheek. "Say the word and he'll never do that again."

Celia shook her head and stepped back so she was in front of the guy sitting on the floor holding his head. "I don't want anybody getting hurt."

Vic stepped to the left so he had a clear shot at the guy on the floor. "Come away with me. With ten grand we could set ourselves up nice."

She lied, told him, "Okay, but don't hurt anyone, please."

He knelt down next to the guy on the floor. "Hear that? She doesn't want anybody hurt. Well, you and I are gonna play a little game, and as long as you let me win, you won't get hurt." Vic poked him in the ribs with the gun. "I'm gonna ask you where Julian's ten thousand is, and I'm gonna hit you with this gun until you tell me or I get tired of the game. And if I don't have the money by then, I'm gonna blow every one of your joints apart, starting with your ankles."

Vic saw motion out of the corner of his eye. Swinging around, raising the gun, he nearly fired.

Celia had come up behind him. She was holding a coat out toward him. "The ten thousand's in one of the pockets."

Jerome pushed himself up into a sitting position, leaning on the wall to steady himself. "You bitch. You've been playing me. And where'd that money come from? He give it to ya, did he?"

Vic was trying to figure out what Jerome was talking about when someone knocked on the door. He figured Julian must've sent someone to check up on him, and if Julian didn't trust him, he was a dead man. He pointed at Celia first then the door.

She yelled, "Go away, we don't want any."

From the hall Vic heard, "It's me, Roy. Open up."

When Celia yelled back that Jerome wasn't there, the guy outside yelled, "Then I'm gonna wait here till he comes back."

Vic pointed the gun at Jerome then at the door.

Jerome yelled, "This isn't a good time, Roy."

"Jerome, you stupid shit, you really fucked up this time."

"Jesus, Roy, keep it down. Somebody's gonna hear you," but Roy went right on yelling. "Go small, I said. Was that so hard to understand? You can't take a hundred thousand from a guy like Julian." After a short pause Roy started up again. "Open up, asshole. I want my half so I can get out of town. I'm not gonna die a miserable death because of you."

Vic thought, "a hundred thousand dollars." That kind of money made it worth taking some big risks, but first he had to make the guy in the hall shut up before one of the neighbors called the cops, so he opened the door and pulled Roy inside, shoving him against the wall then kicking the door closed behind him and holding the gun to his face.

The little, dark-skinned man with a nasty scar over his eye seemed to recognize Vic. "The hell are you doing here?"

As Vic struggled to remember where he'd seen him before, the little guy struggled to get loose. Vic hit him with his gun, hard enough to knock him down. Then Vic worked through what happened to the money, talking through it out loud because that made it easier to figure out. "So you two took the ten grand Manheim owed Julian and bet it on a long shot that paid out a hundred thousand of Julian's own money. I can't believe a couple of bozos like you pulled off something like that."

Then he remembered Celia handing him the coat. She

was still there. He gave her a once-over. "Did you know about the hundred thousand?

"I was going to tell you about it but I didn't get a chance. You're right, that would set us up real nice."

That got a rise out of Jerome. "You whore, I knew you were up to something. You've been planning to run off with him ever since that night Roy hooked you up with him, haven't you?"

Roy yelled at Vic. "Son of a bitch. We figure out the scheme, do all the work, take all the chances, and you take our money. That's not gonna happen."

Vic told them, "Shut up or die, assholes," because he couldn't think with them making noise.

If Vic took the hundred thousand he couldn't leave anybody around to talk, because DeLuca would send an army of goons after him. Vic was working on what to do with Jerome and Roy when someone else knocked on the door. He nodded at Celia then at the door.

She yelled, "Go away."

A voice in the hall yelled, "I'm looking for a guy named Vic."

Vic recognized Julian's voice and panicked, firing his gun through the door, twice. Then he opened the door to drag Julian into the apartment before one of the neighbors came out to see about the gunshots. But as big as Vic was, he still had to use both hands to move the body. He set his gun down on Julian's chest while he dragged him inside.

Roy and Jerome both pounced on Vic as soon as he put his gun down. Still dragging Julian, Vic pushed Roy and Jerome back into the apartment, the two of them hanging onto him like tacklers on a running back. He kicked the door closed and dropped Julian. Then he backed up, smashing Roy and Jerome into the wall behind him, the two of them falling to the floor gasping for breath.

Julian stayed right where Vic dropped him, but Roy and Jerome tried to get back on their feet. Vic's gun had fallen off of Julian's chest and was out of reach, so he hit Roy with an elbow, dropping him like a sack of dirt. Then he decked Jerome with a fist, and was turning around to check on Celia when everything went black.

***

When Celia hit Vic on the back of the head with Joey's new gun he slumped to the floor, as though someone had let the air out of him.

Joey stuck his head in the doorway. "Jesus, Mom, were those gunshots?"

"Bring me some of your dad's dress ties, and hurry."

By the time Joey came with the ties, Julian's lips were blue, as though he'd been swimming in cold water. Celia knew he'd be dead soon, if he wasn't already. She could see the other three breathing but not moving.

When Joey saw the carnage his face went blank, as though a piece of wiring in his brain had burned out. Celia took him by the shoulders and shook him until he looked at her, so she knew the lights had come back on.

He asked her why she wanted the ties.

"Tie 'em up good, hands and feet."

"Dad too?"

"Him especially."

Celia put the coat with the ten thousand in the pocket back in the closet for the police to find. Then she called nine-one-one, ignoring the operator's questions, giving her their address and telling her that someone had just been shot and killed. Then she hung up so she could help Joey.

The job they did tying up the three men wasn't anything to be proud of, but it only needed to hold until the police got there, and she knew they'd be there soon because they liked to appear tough on crime in the projects.

She saw Joey looking at her and he looked scared, the way he looked when he was little and still frightened of things that went bump in the night. Then he was shaking her arm and saying, "Mom," until she came back to the present. She asked him if he had the rest of the hundred thousand. He handed her a roll of cash he fished out of his jacket pocket.

Celia led Joey out into the hallway where he pulled her up short, standing very still, with his head tipped to one side. Then she heard the sirens, too. She took his hand and led him down two flights of stairs to a friend's apartment.

Before she knocked on the door she pulled him around by the shoulders to face her. "We're gonna stay here until the police are gone. And if my friend asks any questions you let me do the talking. The less she knows the better."

"But, won't somebody come looking for the money?"

"I doubt Julian told anybody he was ripped off for a hundred thousand because that would make him look stupid. And Vic didn't find out about it until he heard Roy yelling at Jerome. So I don't think anybody else knows."

"Aren't the police gonna wonder who tied those guys up?"

"Vic will go to prison for killing Julian because his prints are on the gun that killed him. When the police find the ten thousand, they'll assume it was a drug deal that went bad. They probably won't look any further than that, because if they do they'll have to work an open case in the projects, and they hate doing that.

After she knocked on her friend's door, Celia told Joey, "And even if they do come looking for the money, we'll be long gone by morning."

"Where're we gonna go?"

"Someplace where you won't ever need a gun or a lawyer."

ZOMBIES ARE NO LAUGHING MATTER

Laura Canfield, speaking at the Church of the Devine Sepulcher, was five minutes into a touching eulogy for her late husband, J. J., when I heard a distant explosion. At that moment the dearly departed sat bolt upright in his coffin and looked around with the kind of startled expression you'd expect from someone who'd just been poked somewhere inappropriate.

Aside from a couple of gasps and one ear-piercing shriek, the whole church full of mourners just sat there silently gaping at old man Canfield who'd been dead for three days. The mortician had done such a nice job with Canfield's makeup that he looked better than he had when he was alive. So good, I'd wondered if his funeral was just an elaborate hoax when he sat up.

We'd probably all still be there staring at him if he hadn't growled and climbed out of his coffin then stumbled toward his grieving widow with a crazy ravenous look on his face. A few of the mourners had the presence of mind to rush to Laura's aid but they didn't get to her before Canfield did. Laura, enough woman to fill an XXL dress and then some, slapped him so hard he staggered. For a moment he teetered like a drunken sailor. Then, leaning so far in her direction that his weight set him in motion, he lunged at her again. She screamed. Then the dearly departed was all over her.

As he mauled his wife a gorgeous young woman next to me said, "That guy's on her like crows on roadkill."

Having said that loud enough for the people sitting in the next two pews to hear her she added, "He must've been dying to get at her."

I resisted the urge to smile because I didn't want people to think I had enjoyed a comment so insensitive and inappropriate, even if I had.

Crumpling to the floor under J. J.'s weight, Laura flailed at her husband with her fists as he ripped her clothes off with his bare hands. After tearing out a piece of her stomach with his teeth, his head popped up and he looked around at us while he chewed on the bloody viscera dangling from his mouth, and he kept a wary eye on us, like a predator afraid one of us might steal his meal.

A few perverts among the mourners pressed through the crowd to get a better view of Canfield slaughtering his wife, but most of the bereaved ran for the exit at the back of the church. Of course, it didn't do them any good because the church only had one set of doors, and here in Sandy Creek we measure snow in feet. So the doors open in, and with dozens of frantic people crammed against them, there wasn't much chance of anyone getting them open.

Town councilman Andre Reddick tried without any success to coax people away from the doors, and puny Saleem Diaz, the Junior High School English teacher, was beaten by frantic mourners when he tried to push them back. After that, the shouting and shoving degenerated into a free-for-all.

As a distant relative of the deceased I was seated in the second row of pews, which put me close to the action. Unsure of what to do but certain I couldn't just stand there and watch J. J. eat his wife, and intending to help her somehow, I turned to my left. But the pew was so full of people I couldn't get out that way. I turned to my right, which put me face to face with the beautiful young woman who'd made the tasteless roadkill remark.

Illogically, especially given the dreadful situation, I started to apologize to her, even though I hadn't done anything wrong. But then her beautiful dark eyes stared into mine, triggering the exasperating mental paralysis I always suffer when confronted by a beautiful woman.

She nodded in Laura's direction and asked, "You think she's still alive?"

Helplessly distracted by her shimmering, wavy black hair and flawless dark skin, I had only half-heard the words her seductively fine mouth had shaped.

She touched my arm and said, "I asked you if you think she's still alive."

I shook my head. "It looks like she stopped fighting."

Leaning so close to me I smelled the sweet scent of her hair and felt the warmth of her breath on my ear, she whispered, "She doesn't have the stomach for it."

"Get it?" she said, elbowing me and grinning. "She doesn't have the stomach for it?"

I smiled. Then she smiled, and her smile made me feel so good I wanted to take it home. But it was watching her lips as she talked that really drove me crazy. I imagined kissing them. Then I imagined doing other things to her and was glad she couldn't read my mind.

"I figured out what that looks like," she said, pointing at Laura then scrunching up her face as though she'd tasted something bad. "A blender drink made out of a meat-lover's pizza."

I told her that her comment was in poor taste then immediately regretted it, but she didn't seem to take offense. It wasn't until she smiled and said, "Poor Taste. Nice come back," that I realized I'd made a bad joke of it.

She held her hand out to me. "My name's Willow, and no tree jokes, please. I've heard them all."

As I took her delicate-looking little hand in mine and told her to call me Brad, Arnie Levesque, the owner of the funeral home handling Mr. Canfield's service, walked up behind her. Arnie, who had changed his name to Armand years ago because he didn't think the name Arnie sounded sophisticated enough for a funeral director, had come to tell Willow, "You really should show some respect for the dead and grieving, especially in a house of worship."

She spun around to answer him, turning her back to me, and I eyed her shamelessly. Slender as a twig but deliciously curved, her body aroused a desire in me so prurient, that even if I'd had the words to describe it I wouldn't have had the courage to say them to her.

While I groped her visually, Willow asked Levesque, "Do you really think Canfield or his wife care what I say about them now?"

Arnie scowled at her.

In a defiantly loud voice she told him, "I think they should rename this place 'Casa Del Corpse,'" at which Arnie turned bright red then stormed off muttering things that sounded suspiciously like obscenities.

Willow yelled after him, "How about 'Casa Del Carcass,' you like that better?"

Then she turned around to face me again and said, "Now where were we?"

I told her, "Arnie would have embalmed Canfield, so there's no way he's alive."

She told me. "I'm going to change my will to stipulate an open coffin so I can scare the shit out of my relatives."

Before I respond my attention was drawn back to the grisly spectacle of Canfield gnawing on his wife because the sound of him slobbering over her entrails had been replaced by loud, aggressive snarling, as though someone had taken an ill-tempered dog's favorite bone.

Sonny Peterson, a big burly car salesman and former high school football star, had caused the commotion by prying the old man off of his wife. He managed to hold J. J.'s growling, thrashing corpse away from Laura for a few moments. But when

Canfield got a mouthful of Sonny's arm, Sonny let the old man go and backed away, and old man Canfield went back to eating his wife, enthusiastically ripping out another piece of Laura's insides with his teeth.

With my insides churning at the sight, Willow's next comment sounded disturbingly nonchalant. "The guy's like a kid on a sugar high tearing open his Christmas presents."

With most of Laura's insides outside, J. J. slobbered blood all over her dress and his suit while he gnawed on a piece of intestine. I had foolishly considered helping poor Laura, but if Sonny, who was twice my size, couldn't hold onto Canfield's corpse without being bit, I certainly couldn't.

Just then, a man wearing overalls forced his way through the knot of people gawking at the grisly spectacle. Judging by his well-worn working man's clothes, long hair, and bushy beard, I figured he was probably one of the local survivalists we occasionally hear about but rarely see.

A big, heavy-set guy whose beard hid his facial features except for his flattened nose and gray eyes, he walked right up behind Canfield, pulled out a handgun and shot him in the head. When the old man's corpse rolled off of Laura, he shot her in the head too.

Sonny, who was holding his bloody arm, yelled, "Jesus, Ruben."

After glancing at Sonny's arm Ruben asked him what had happened.

Sonny had barely gotten out the words, "He bit me," before Ruben shot him in the head.

The crowd gave Ruben lots of room while he looked the rest of us over. Apparently satisfied that none of us had been bitten, he explained why he'd shot Laura and Sonny. "I knew when I saw Canfield sit up he was one of the Devil's disciples, and when nobody else did anything I knew it was up to me. As for Laura, I put her out of her misery. And as for Sonny, if you get bit by one of them, you become one of them."

A woman somewhere in the back of the crowd yelled,

"Isn't anyone going to arrest him?"

"So Ruben," Willow said, frowning as though deep in thought, "why would the Devil make old man Canfield eat his wife?"

Apparently Ruben thought Willow actually believed his nonsense because he spouted more senseless drivel with the enthusiasm of a religious fanatic. "The end times are upon us. That's when God, the Devil, and the Antichrist finally slug it out. The Devil's bringing back the dead to kill us because all of us humans will side with either God or the Antichrist."

I asked him if by end times he meant Armageddon.

Ruben shook his head. "You obviously don't know your scripture. Armageddon's a place. It's where the armies of the Messiah, the Antichrist, and Satan gather for the final battle. 'And behold, the Devil shall resurrect a great host of the dead and their multitudes shall cover the land.'"

With a wry smile Willow whispered to me, "Old man Canfield may not have had the land covered, but he was all over his wife."

I asked Ruben if he really believed J. J. was one of the Devil's soldiers.

"You think the Devil's going to raise an army by opening a recruiting center at the mall?"

I told him I hadn't thought about it. He told me I should. I lied, told him I would.

Then a little old woman, a stick figure with a wrinkled face and tufts of wispy-thin, white hair spotting her head stepped out of the crowd.

Like a mother scolding a naughty kid she grabbed Ruben's ear and told him, "You put that gun away this minute."

Ruben begged the old woman to let go of his ear.

When she did, Willow asked him, "You really think God and the Devil chose to have it out right here in beautiful Cornhusk, Iowa?"

When Ruben said, "And the non-believers shall perish," the old woman reached for his ear again.

Ruben got away from her by ducking into the crowd. Willow told me he was a casualty of his beliefs. I told her he was certifiable.

"Hey," she said, as though I had insulted her, "I've dated worse guys than that."

I immediately began daydreaming about dating Willow, but my fantasy was cut short by a very upset young girl with sun-bleached hair and a freckle-covered face.

She had stepped forward holding a cell phone to ask the crowd, "Has anyone got decent reception?"

After a few mumbled answers a tall, thin, nerdy-looking kid stepped forward. "There's only one cell tower on this side of town and it's probably down or overloaded. You might have to go all the way to Vermilion to get another tower."

"So what the hell are we supposed to do?" the girl demanded, glaring at him as though it was his fault.

"There's nothing you can do but wait a while and try it again."

She tried it again without waiting, and it obviously didn't work because she told the kid she hated him, which he seemed to take personally. After that, an eerie, tense silence settled in the church.

Willow caught me staring at her and I blushed like a little boy, which made her smile. I wondered if she was amused by my discomfort or happy knowing I enjoyed looking at her. Fortunately a commotion in the back of the church saved me from having to explain myself.

Someone had finally gotten one of the doors open and a badly decomposed former human had burst into the church and grabbed a young boy. Then all at the same time: the guy who had opened the door tried to close it; the kid tried to break free; a woman began screaming, and one of the other kids nearby said to the corpse, "Uncle Ted, is that you?"

Several people near the door forced it shut. Two men went to the kid's aid but couldn't break the murderous thing's grip. While they struggled with it, it tried to bite the closest piece of exposed flesh. The action was fast and confusing and looked as though it would end badly for the kid, until a very small and very wrinkled old woman came up behind the thing and grabbed its head with both hands. Where her fingers touched its parchment-like skin, it sizzled and burned like raw meat on a hot barbeque grill.

As the heinous thing thrashed and flailed, it let out a scream that sounded as though it had come right out of hell. And although it was so strong two men had had trouble restraining it, it couldn't break away from the old lady's grasp. Being a well-educated firm believer in the sanctity of science, if someone had told me when I left for the funeral this morning that I'd see a witch this afternoon, I'd have laughed at the idea, but I couldn't think of any other way to explain it.

When the old woman let go of the creature it slumped to the floor in a pile, like a marionette with its strings cut. A woman came and led the kid away while the two stunned men stared slack-jawed at the old lady.

So stooped over she was no taller than the boy, and so skinny she barely had a third dimension, the old woman told the two men gawking at her, "Well you two pussies weren't getting it done."

Then she looked around at the group. They all looked stunned. I know I was.

"Name's Althea," she said, "and I'm the sweet little lady who lives next door to you."

When I told her I doubted it, she lunged at me, her hands reaching for my face. I ducked. She managed to touch my face anyway. I cringed. She let out a big, unladylike laugh and Willow laughed with her.

When I'd recovered my breath well enough to talk I pointed at the creature on the floor and asked the old lady how she had burned it with her bare hands.

"I dipped them in the holy water."

Someone asked her how she knew the holy water would work.

Considering the risk she'd taken, her answer was surprisingly matter-of-fact and her attitude remarkably blasé. "Because Ruben said they were the devil's disciples."

I told her she was crazy for grabbing something so deadly just on Ruben's say so. She called me a sissy. It's harsh when an old lady calls you a sissy, but having to admit that Ruben, one of the nut-job survivalists I'd been laughing at for years, might have been right all along somehow felt worse. I started to worry about my odds of surviving in a world being fought over by God and the devil.

Now that the thing was dead, or whatever it is you call it when one of those things stops moving, we all crowded around to inspect it. Unlike old man Canfield, the clothes on this corpse were no more than shreds of cloth with clumps of soil, a variety of live bugs, and a few worms clinging to them. Where its skin showed, it was leathery and brown and stretched tightly over its bones. Where its bones showed, they were chalky-white and shiny.

A woman standing nearby asked, "Where the hell did that come from?"

Ruben had rejoined us. Raising his arms like a tent preacher, he proclaimed, "And the dead shall walk among you."

I guessed people were becoming inured to his insanity because I didn't hear any derisive remarks this time.

During the tense silence that followed his comment, Willow fired a broadside at director Levesque who was standing on the other side of the prostrate carcass. "Either this one's been in the ground a while, or you did a lousy job prepping him."

Arnie scowled. Willow smiled.

Joe Finch, a clean-shaven, young ex-marine, who worked as a janitor at the Sandy Creek Federal Credit Union, stepped forward and announced that he would, "see if the coast is clear."

A stocky, dark-complexioned man with a dimpled chin and eyebrows that reminded me of a bird's wings, Joe dragged a table holding a stack of funeral programs over under one of the two-story stained glass windows. The place became deathly silent as we all watched him climb up on the table to peer outside.

While we waited anxiously for his report I heard a commotion behind me. The girl with the cell phone and the boy who'd been attacked were fighting over the bowl of holy water on the altar. The boy pulled steadily on the bowl and would have won if the girl hadn't yanked on it. I watched it fall and its contents splash on the floor, the antique wooden floorboards greedily soaking up the precious fluid.

The kids looked startled then guilty then scared, no doubt afraid that they were in a lot of trouble. I too was scared, because ever since Althea had showed us the effect of God's water on those monsters, I'd been counting on using it if any more of them showed up. I just couldn't visualize any of the people there for J.J. Canfield's funeral service as corpse fighters.

At that moment Willow, who'd stuck to me like a bad debt, said, "Ah, shit," so convincingly I thought some of those things had broken in. I looked around anxiously. Satisfied we didn't have any more of the former cemetery tenants among us, I asked her what was wrong.

She seemed surprised by my question, asked me, "Didn't you see the dirt on that thing?"

I nodded my head. I'd seen the dirt, but didn't see her point.

She announced that, "It must have come from the bone zone," as though it explained everything.

"The what?"

"You know. The bone zone. The graveyard. What planet have you been living on?"

Then she asked the group, "Does anybody know how many bodies are buried out there?"

They all shook their heads or shrugged their shoulders or just stood there looking dazed, except for Joe, who was still up on the table. He said, "Judging from the gravestones, there must be a hundred, give or take."

A very excited teenage boy with a bad case of acne told

us to look at the stained glass window above Joe. The top of the glass panel depicted light and dark angels in a cosmic struggle. The middle portion was a sadistic, allegorical depiction of a battle between humans and skeletons that looked ominously like the thing lying at our feet. The losers, some of them humans, some of them skeletons, were falling into a flaming pit at the base of the panel.

With great solemnity Willow announced, "Those things may not be as bad for you as you think."

I told her she was crazy.

When she grinned I knew she'd set me up. "How bad can they be? They're free-range organic zombies."

The nerd chose that moment to share a little more knowledge with us. "That faint boom we heard when Canfield's wife was giving the eulogy may have been an atmospheric detonation of a thermonuclear device."

A man in the back of the crowd yelled, "How about saying that again in English."

The kid frowned in the guy's general direction, but to his credit he did try to explain. "When a nuke is exploded above ground it sends out a ginormous magnetic pulse that induces power surges in electronic devices. One energy surge from one bomb can burn out all of the electronics for hundreds, maybe thousands, of miles. Some nukes are designed and targeted specifically to knock out the enemy's electronic infrastructure."

The guy in the back yelled, "You twit. That's not English."

The kid rolled his eyes. "None of your radios, televisions, cars, trains, airplanes, phones, or anything else with electronics in it will ever work again."

The freckled, cell-phone-addicted, teenaged girl pushed through the crowd and demanded, "How are my friends gonna know what I'm doing if I can't post anything?"

When the kid told her, "Your friends have bigger problems," she threw her phone at him and stormed off.

A true nerd, he failed to catch it. It glanced off his chest then clattered across the floor, stopping when it hit Ruben's left foot. He looked at it curiously then announced, "If someone did use a nuke on us, it was the false prophet, the antichrist. And it's either that Russian nut-job, Putin, or some Islamic extremist in the Middle East."

Ignoring Ruben's outburst, Willow asked the nerd, "If the electricity's out, there won't be any water either, will there?"

He shook his head.

"Oh, well that's just great," she said, pointing at the creature on the floor. "So pretty soon we're all gonna smell like that thing."

When a woman in the crowd said, "I'm more afraid of being eaten," Willow leaned in close to me and asked if I was getting hungry.

In spite of not having had any food for the better part of the day I shook my head, because after watching old man Canfield gnaw on his wife the thought of eating made me nauseous.

Willow said, "I sure could use a bite" then smiled impishly.

I thought she looked positively erotic. I told her she was heartless.

"No," she said, "Mrs. Canfield's heartless."

I asked her if it would it kill her to show a little respect for the dead.

"Oh sure," she said, "you get all indignant when I crack a joke, but you're just as bad."

I asked her what she meant.

"Kill me," she said, "you asked if it would kill me."

I was about to tell her that she was giving me credit for things I'd said accidentally, when we were interrupted by a woman with two noisy kids in tow who walked up to Miss Enright, the organist for the funeral. The woman asked Enright to play something gentle to soothe her children.

Miss Enright, who seemed less than enthusiastic, told her, "All I know are hymns."

"Then play something upbeat, something that will get their minds off what's happening."

Miss Enright, dressed all in black old-lady funeral attire, wiggled her plentiful butt as she planted it on the organ bench. Then, pounding on the keys with all the stops out, she broke into a booming, off-key rendition of *Onward Christian Soldiers*.

Part way through the first verse I heard banging on the church doors and a chorus of growling that seemed to respond to Miss Enright's own howling. She stopped and the noise soon abated. Everyone there was looking at the doors. I wondered if they'd all had the same terrifying thoughts I'd had - that more of those things had showed up for the party, that they had us trapped in the church, that they could break through the doors at any moment, and that they wanted to eat us.

Willow chose that moment to be wildly inappropriate. "Gee, it sounds like a real Zombie-Fest out there, a good old-fashioned Graveyard-Gala, a real Bone-Bash, a Gore-Fest..."

I pleaded with her to stop. She laughed. I noticed people were looking at her as though she was insane, which I suspected was at least partially true, and which for some strange reason made her seem even more attractive.

Someone asked Joe what was going on outside. When he turned around to give us an update, the color had drained from his face. "We've got company."

Althea asked him how many.

"I can't see how many are at the doors, but there's a dozen or more headed this way from the cemetery, and there's more coming out of the ground."

Willow asked the group, "Did anyone else notice that those things stopped making a racket when Miss Enright stopped singing, or whatever that was she was doing.

When a very indignant Miss Enright assured us that it had been a coincidence Willow suggested, "Then sing a little more of that song for us, and really belt it out this time. We'll see if that's what got them upset."

No sooner had Miss Enright begun to screech out another verse than I heard renewed pounding and growling over her jarring vocals. An indignant-looking Miss Enright pushed away from the organ and scowled at us.

Althea, bless her empathetic little heart, suggested, "Maybe they like Miss Enright's singing."

Willow said, "Gee, I don't know. Althea, I think they probably wanted to kill her. It sounded that good."

As a kindness to Miss Enright I suggested, "Maybe they're staunch atheists and the Christian lyrics upset them," but I suspected Willow was right - that Miss Enright's singing was killing them.

Then we heard from Ruben. Having been dismissed as a crackpot earlier, I think he wanted to rub our noses in it. "And behold a mighty host shall rise up out of the earth and smite the nonbelievers."

His mother slapped the back of his head. "How many times do I have to tell you? If you talk like that people are gonna lock you up."

The nerd suggested, "Maybe we should be quiet and see if the creatures go away," but Joe said, "I'm worried about the doors holding," and that got everyone stirred up again.

Well, everyone except for Willow who leaned over and asked me, "You thinking what I'm thinking?"

When I told her I seriously doubted it she pouted. She actually looked hurt. So I apologized. She grinned. Then I felt like a fool, but relieved that I hadn't hurt her feelings.

Predictably unpredictable, Willow said she had a question for me.

Wary of another wisecrack, I cautiously asked her, "What?"

"If one of them gets a hard-on, do you call it a boner, or would that be politically incorrect?"

She giggled, then leaned close to my ear and whispered, "I wish someone would jump my bones."

There was nothing I wanted more than to jump her bones, and hoping her comment had been a thinly-veiled invitation, I played along. "You know, it's not just the dead that want to jump your bones."

"Well I should hope not," she said, affectedly, "'cause those things are gutless."

She elbowed me and asked if I got it.

I closed my eyes and hung my head.

"Besides," she said, "they're not what you'd call deep thinkers, are they?"

"So you prefer the cerebral type?" I asked, feigning astonishment.

"I want a guy I can have an intelligent conversation with when we're not engaged in wild salacious sex."

The thought of having wild salacious sex with her excited me a lot more than I dared to let on, so I tried to make a joke of it. "You actually come up for air?"

"Girl's gotta breathe," she said.

Then she stared off into space, as though she was contemplating one of the questions that had stumped the great philosophers. "But I also like a guy with a sense of humor."

I told her that a guy would have to have a sense of humor to date her. She called me a hypocrite. I asked her why. She asked me if I'd ever eaten raw fish at a Sushi bar. I was wondering what that had to do with a sense of humor when she asked me if I'd ever had Steak Tartar.

I asked her if we could change the subject because my stomach wasn't ready for food jokes. She promised me she would if I answered her about the Steak Tartar. I told her I'd tried it once but didn't like it.

"Well, there you go," she said, decisively.

"Really," I said, "that makes me a hypocrite? Hell, I barely choked down the first forkful, and unlike old man Canfield who ate his own wife while she was still alive, I didn't bite the cow before they killed it."

Willow told me to, "Lurch a mile in his shoes."

I reminded her that she'd promised to change the subject.

Saying, "I may have lied, Brad," she batted her eyelashes at me coquettishly.

Then Joe asked the group, "Are we just gonna wait for

them to break the doors down?"

With the passion of a televangelist Ruben declared, "It is written that the Antichrist's army will burn in hell."

One of the women said what I suspect we were all thinking. "You're full of shit, Ruben."

"His response, "We'll lure them into the church and set fire to it," was met with mumbled skepticism.

"Don't you get it?" he said. "If it's written in the bible that the Devil and his army burn in the fires of hell, then that's what's gotta happen."

When a man in the back asked, "We're not really gonna risk our lives doing what this nut job says, are we?" Willow told him, "I think Ruben may be on to something."

When the cell phone girl's mother told Willow, "You're as crazy as he is," Willow said, "Come on, you gotta admit, living in Sandy Creek can be hell."

Ruben asked the group if anyone had a better idea. His question was met with silence, except for Joe who asked him, "And what happens to us when those things pile in here?"

Andre, the town councilman, proposed luring the creatures into the rows of pews. "It'll slow them down. If we wait in the aisle on the other side of the room we should have time to get around them, and we could set fire to the place on our way out."

Joe pointed out that if we set fire to the church we'd have nowhere left to hide.

Althea surprised everyone by taking Ruben's side. "Sorry, Joe, but we're running out of time, so unless you've got something better, I say we go with what Ruben and Andre suggested. And if no one objects, I think Andre should be in charge."

Althea's endorsement having settled the debate, Andre asked for volunteers. Someone asked him what they'd have to do.

"We'll stay behind to get the bonfire in place and light it."

Willow asked Andre what he wasn't telling us.

"If people are slow getting out, we'll have to hold those things back."

A woman standing behind me muttered, "Only a fool would volunteer for something like that."

So naturally, I raised my hand. As one of the few adult males in the group I knew I'd be drafted if I didn't volunteer. I figured I might as well be a hero if I had to do it anyway, and I thought it might earn me some points with Willow.

After telling me I was nuts, Willow asked, "Did you volunteer just to get away from me?"

When I shook my head she raised her hand. That earned her some surprised looks but I think people were happy to have volunteers no matter who they were, because it let them off the hook. Andre asked for more volunteers. An awkward silence followed during which most of the people looked away, like high school kids who didn't want to be called on by their teacher.

Ira Levinson, an early-twenty-something young man sporting an immaculately trimmed beard and a designer suit that showed off his very athletic-looking physique, was the only person to step forward. Including Andre, that made four fools.

Instead of insisting on more volunteers, which is what I would've done, Andre addressed the crowd. "If we're going to hold those things back while you make your escape we'll need weapons. We can use table legs for clubs, but they'll be more effective if we make torches out of them. So we'll need clothing for rags and something combustible to douse them with. So if you've got anything combustible, we need it. And we'll need stuff for the bonfire too."

Donations included a cigarette lighter and a pocket-sized can of lighter fluid, courtesy of Ruben, and such clothing as wasn't needed for modesty.

In the midst of our search for stuff to burn, Willow, who had stuck with me like gum on a shoe, asked me, "What do you call a bunch of zombies at work?"

I asked her if she had ever sought professional help.

After blurting out, "A skeleton crew" she laughed

uncontrollably.

I told her there were public assistance programs if she couldn't afford the cost of a psychiatrist.

"Oh, eat me," she said, then laughed so hard she had trouble getting her breath back.

I told her she should whisper if she couldn't control herself.

"You know," she said, suddenly very serious, but still much too loud, "you'd be better at this whole Zombie thing if you boned up on them."

Feigning exasperation, I rolled my eyes at her. Judging from the sounds she was making she was trying not to choke.

For the fire we collected two long wooden tables, several dozen hymnals, the guest book and leftover programs for Canfield's funeral, and the family pictures Canfield's wife had brought. To force the zombies into the pews, Andre had us overturn the tables and set them to the sides of the doorway before we piled the stuff on them. Later we'd slide them into place to block their exit. And all the while we had listened to the incessant pounding and strange guttural noises made by the creatures trying to get in.

Working under the possibly erroneous assumption that fire would be an effective weapon against the zombies, Andre gave Ira, Willow, and me each a torch. Then we held a little torch lighting ceremony. Ira stood with Andre and Willow stood next to me, and we waited for everyone to get in place on the other side of the church. My stomach fluttering like a pennant in a windstorm as I wondered if those things would be able to smell us, or sense us, or detect us in some weird zombie sort of way as they stumbled past us.

Willow muttered, "My momma didn't raise me just to be part of some boneyard banquet."

Andre took a final look around then flipped the bolt latch that had been holding the doors closed. Taking my cue from him I pulled our door open, swinging it around to hide Willow and me. Standing very close to Willow I was tempted to get fresh with her, but the guttural slobbering of several dozen zombies lumbering past us took the edge off my desire.

When the sounds of their shuffling feet had moved away from us I took a chance and peered around the edge of the door. The dreadful things were swarming through the church like a crowd of stoned bargain hunters at a Black Friday sale. If one of them fell down, the ones behind it trampled its carcass. As the downed zombies struggled to get up they got tangled up with the creatures stumbling over them, creating squirming piles of partially-putrefied remains.

When the foul, snarling things were little more than a boney arm's length away from the people cowering on the far side of the room Andre yelled, "Run."

The dumb but deadly things attempted to turn around between the pews when they saw their dinners getting away, causing a large creature-jam.

I saw one of the things pull Ruben's mother down. It ripped a chunk of her loose, chewing on the still partially attached piece of flesh while more of the things fell on her. Ruben shot four or five of them in the head before he ran out of ammunition. By then his mother had almost disappeared under a squirming mass of the things, like a mouse that had stumbled into a nest of snakes.

It was suicidal, but Ruben stayed and beat the things with his empty gun until the corpse of some kid's grandmother sank its teeth into his arm. Ruben bashed the thing's face in with his gun, but not before more creatures tore into him. He collapsed after one of them ripped his jugular open with its teeth. We could only watch as the fiends fed on him and the withered flesh of his mother.

The rest of the fleeing mourners made it to the exit. But they made a lot of noise, which got the attention of the zombies that weren't feasting on Ruben and his mother, and the horde of unholy dead began lumbering toward the exit and us.

As the last mourners made their way out, Andre and Ira and Willow and I slid the two tables piled with flammable debris into a "V" and lit them. Too stupid to go around the fire, the partially decomposed humans amassed on the other side of the pyre. As more of the things came for us, they pressed against the ones nearest the fire, pushing some of them into it, their corpses temporarily smothering the flames, creating paths of gore for the ones behind them. So, although our funeral pyre had become a wall of flames, snarling human remains began stumbling out of the smoke, kicking up sparks as they emerged, looking like Ruben's devil's regiment.

A soldier will fall on barbed wire so his comrades can get over it before the enemy's machine guns mow them down. The zombies exhibited no such altruism - the ones barbequed in our bonfire were simply pushed into it by the ravenous mob behind them. In fact, I might have had some compassion for the squirming tangle of toasted carcasses if the foul things had considered me anything more than human sushi. The irony wasn't lost on me – we were about to become raw dinners for well-done diners.

I downed my first zombie by stabbing it with my lit torch and shoving it back against the ones behind it. Dry spots on the shredded remnants of its decayed flesh and rotted clothes burst into flames leaving a slimy mass of molten zombie goo on my torch that looked like melted dark-brown plastic. The flailing, screaming thing stumbled and fell and was immediately replaced by another.

When I dared glance away I checked on my fellow volunteers. Willow was struggling but okay. I had stayed close to her so I could keep the toughest looking zombies away from her. As for Ira, fleeting glimpses of a bloody knit shirt were all I saw of him. I hoped he hadn't suffered much. His demise left just Andre and Willow and I to hold back the swarm of bloodthirsty devils.

Because of the thick putrid smoke rising from the burning zombies I could barely see Andre, who wasn't more than ten feet from me. The next time I glanced his way I saw a creature leap on his back. Andre spun around but the dead thing held on, sinking its teeth into his shoulder like a wolf bringing down a deer. When I looked back moments later, two more creatures were on him. I needed to get Willow out of there.

I shoved the zombie impaled on my torch away with my foot. It stumbled backwards, the torch sliding out of its stomach with a sickly, slurping sound. It crashed into the one behind it and both of them staggered backwards into the fire. One burst into flames immediately. It wouldn't be coming out. With a hungry predatory look on its blackened face, and smelling like burnt meat, the other one lunged at me. I held my torch out. The fiend impaled itself, pressing against the torch so hard I felt something in its stomach burst.

As we struggled, suspended in a terrifying embrace, it growled and gnashed its teeth and dribbled streams of bloody drool on me, and even with my torch embedded deep in its stomach the thing put up a fierce fight. Having a face inches from your own that's nothing but bone and sinew and dried blood with a few shreds of skin and trying to bite you is terrifying.

When the fight finally went out of the thing and it crumpled like a broken Halloween toy I shoved a pathetic-looking creature away from Willow. I shoved her outside then yanked the door closed behind me.

The people milling about outside the church looked surprised to see us. They asked about Andre and Ira. The bad news started an intense argument among them over what our next move should be.

I took stock of our situation. My clothes were splattered with zombie guts and my hands were slick with the gruesome goo. Every part of my body ached. Worst of all, our comrades who'd died in the fight would soon join the ranks of the reanimated, and I didn't relish staking them.

The way I saw it we only had two choices. We could stay in our cars and wait for help that might not come. And if we spent the night in our cars, we'd be trapped without food or water. Or we could walk the six miles back to town. No telling what we'd find there or how many of those things we'd encounter on the way. And while we walked, we'd have no place to hide or put up a defense.

But for me it was no-brainer because I wanted answers to some big questions, like: is God really at war with the devil, and if so, why here, for Christ's sake? And what would I have to do to get back in his good graces? And why in hell did I have to meet the girl of my dreams at a time like this?

I knew I wouldn't find the answers by hiding in my car so I voted for walking back to town. Most of the others wanted to know what was happening elsewhere in the world and voted with me. When they headed toward town Willow and I walked together at the back of the group. I asked her how she was coping.

She frowned then sighed heavily, as though distressed, "The world's changed, Brad." Then she grinned at me and asked, "You know how I can tell?"

I braced myself for something outlandish. "I give up, Willow. How can you tell the world has changed?"

"Because no one's going to say 'bite me' or 'eat me' ever again."

For the first time in my life I was able to look a beautiful girl right in the eye, and without even a hint of embarrassment, tell her how I felt. "I really like you, Willow."

I had walked several feet past her before I realized she'd stopped. When I turned around she was looking at her feet and her head was tipped as though she was lost in thought. Then with a shrug of her slender shoulders, she came and took my hand and asked me, "What's a zombie's favorite rhythm?"

Before I could answer she said, "A deadbeat" then laughed.

Even though a lot of the stuff that had happened that day belonged in the column labeled "Horrible," the day had ended up in the plus column because I'd met Willow, and as long as she was with me I didn't much care what we found up ahead.

A PHOTOGRAPHIC MEMORY

I thought I heard someone call my name, but when I looked around to see who it was, no one in the coffee shop seemed interested in me. That's when I spotted him. A vaguely familiar looking guy in line behind me.

It happens to all of us at some time or other. You see someone who looks familiar but you can't remember how you know them. If you're like me and you've got something to hide, the sight of someone like that is especially troubling.

Every day I look forward to stopping for a latte on my way to work, and starting my day with Lauren, my clandestine lover, an irresistible married woman who lives in apartment 12B one floor above me.

No doubt I was making something out of nothing. He was probably just a guy from my apartment building or someone from another department I passed in the hall at work one day. But now I can't possibly relax until I figure out how I know the guy.

I found a table near the back of the room but sat facing the counter to I could watch the man from an unknown part of my life. He didn't have the dark sinister looks of a killer from a Film Noir, my favorite movie genre. In fact, nothing about the man seemed threatening.

The man was wearing a nondescript dark business suit, white shirt, and red tie, much like the clothes I had on. And yet, I sensed danger in his presence, my breath coming in small quick bursts, my muscles taut.

He was either younger than me, or had better genes, because he had considerably more hair and considerably less gray. And while my gray hair aged my appearance, his gave him an air of refinement and wisdom, the kind coveted by politicians.

I had the wild thought that he might be a celebrity with a dark past, someone I'd seen in a news broadcast. But much as I liked that thought, I couldn't shake the feeling that he was somehow part of my life.

The clerk didn't put a lid on his coffee which meant he'd be staying to drink it, so I averted my face enough to see him but not be seen by him. Like a deer watching a predator, I eyed him warily as he took his drink to a table on the far side of the room.

Even though I'd be late for work if I didn't leave soon, I didn't dare stand up for fear the movement would draw his attention and expose me to his scrutiny. As minutes ticked by, my breathing became shallower, my heart beat faster, and I felt unpleasantly warm.

When I could no longer stand the suspense, I resolved to confront him, to go over there and grill him with questions until I knew why his presence caused me so much anxiety.

I boldly slid my chair back to stand up then immediately lost my nerve. I made two more abortive attempts to face him before resigning myself to my cowardice. Wishing I had a newspaper to hide behind, I put a hand up to hide my face.

While I struggled to place the man, I spotted movement out of the corner of my eye. Glancing furtively in his direction I saw him get up to leave. Like a pardoned death-row prisoner, I was enormously relieved that the ordeal would end soon, but then he walked toward me rather than the exit. The world fell out from under my poor stomach. Like a scared kid pulling his blanket up to hide from the monster in his room, I looked away and hoped for a miracle.

His question, "Do I know you?" had a disturbingly accusatory tone to it.

Standing just two feet from me, he must have seen my hands shaking. And when I replied, "I don't think so," I was sure he could hear my voice falter.

He didn't leave, just stood there by my chair staring at me. His look darkened, his frown deepened, and he squinted at me. My safety depended on placing him before he placed me. I was sure of it. So I willed my mind to locate him among a lifetime of memories.

While I struggled with that, he pressed his case. "I'm sure we've met."

Afraid my voice might give away my identity, I just shook my head. He tipped his head as though he didn't believe me. During the awkward silence that followed it occurred to me that maybe I couldn't place him because he'd aged since I'd seen him last.

I'm not sure how things would've worked out if Lauren hadn't come into the shop. When she spotted me she smiled and headed my way. While she carefully threaded her way through the tables in the crowded room, the man standing next to me had his back to her.

I knew from the moment I saw Lauren, were I'd seen the guy standing over me threateningly. It was her smile that did it, the smile on the bride's face in the wedding picture Lauren kept on her bedside table, the one that always left me feeling guilty. That's where I'd seen him. He was the young groom in her wedding picture.

He spun around when Lauren said, "Hi, Sweetheart," to me.

I suppose he recognized his wife's voice. If she'd played along, pretended she knew it was him, all would be well now, but she stopped short when he turned around, probably assuming from his dark countenance that he'd figured out what was going on between us.

I could've saved the day, could've said something clever, something to suggest that his wife was just a casual acquaintance. And I might have done that if a wild thought hadn't struck me just then. I hesitated as I tried to dismiss it, the delay putting the last nail in the coffin of Lauren's marriage. But what if my crazy thought wasn't crazy after all? What if I looked familiar, but not familiar enough to place because I'd aged ten years since my wedding picture was taken, the one my wife kept on our bedside table?

HIGH SCHOOL HIJINKS

Kevin, who had been standing in the hallway leaning against his locker waiting for the bell to signal the end of lunch period, turned around when he heard a soft, tentative voice behind him say his name.

A dark complexioned girl with delicately perfect looks and shoulder-length, jet-black hair that shimmered in the glare of the overhead lights was looking at him expectantly. He'd seen her before, had always thought she looked better than any high school girl had a right to look.

As she held her hand out to Kevin, a hugely unpopular boy named Marty, appeared behind her shaking his head vigorously, obviously trying to warn Kevin about something. Ignoring him, Kevin took the girl's hand in his, and as he enjoyed the warmth and tenderness of her touch, he wondered what she could possibly want with him.

Looking into her bright gray eyes as her lips formed the words, "My name's Gina," Kevin felt self-conscious and awkward and special all at the same time.

And when she said to him, "I hear you're really smart," he felt a surge of pride to think she actually knew him for his smarts. But it was so unexpected that all he thought to say was, "Thanks."

She told him she'd be really grateful if he'd help her with her algebra, and that she'd pay him ten dollars an hour. He didn't care about the money and was about to tell her as much, but before he found the nerve to answer her, she told him, "Pick me up at my house at eight" and walked away, disappearing around a corner.

"Don't say I didn't warn you."

It was Marty. Kevin asked him what the hell he wanted.

"That's badass Billy Rizzo's girlfriend."

Kevin told Marty, "Not my problem."

Marty told Kevin, "Yeah it is, 'cause he's coming this way and he looks seriously pissed."

Sure enough Kevin spotted a big glowering hulk of a boy headed toward him, forcing his way through the mass of kids clogging the hall. Kevin had heard about Billy; heard how he'd bloodied kids just for the fun of it. And from the look on Billy's face, Kevin was pretty sure that's what Billy had in mind for him.

Stopping in front of Kevin, Billy loomed over him, blocking out the overhead light like a sinister cloud. After poking Kevin in the chest hard enough to leave a bruise Billy told him, "I'm gonna kick the shit out of you."

Kevin knew that if he backed down the whole school would hear about it by morning and that he'd never live it down. But standing there at eye level with Billy's massive neck, Kevin did, just for a moment, consider making a run for it rather than get pounded.

Saying, "You asked for it, punk," loud enough to draw a crowd around them, Billy took a big roundhouse swing at Kevin, who watched with horror as Billy's fist came toward his face.

"Don't do it," a deep booming voice yelled.

Billy pulled his punch, missing Kevin's face, but coming close enough for Kevin to feel a puff of air as it passed.

The voice that had stopped it belonged to Mr. Taylor, the school's guidance counselor. He had walked up behind Billy. "It'll be your third suspension this year. You'll be expelled."

Billy poked Kevin in the chest again then opened his

mouth as if to say something but didn't. A moment or two later, looking confused and frustrated, Billy blurted out, "You'll be sorry" before storming off.

Kevin watched him disappear into the crush of onlookers who'd gathered around them, no doubt to watch Kevin get bloodied. He really did want to spend time with Gina, couldn't think of anything he wanted more. But he also knew he couldn't hope for anything more than a purely platonic relationship with her. Was he dumb enough to risk being beaten to a pulp just for a few minutes with her?

"You're a real fool, Kevin Blake." It was Marty again. He sounded as though he was having difficulty holding back a laugh when he said, "A girl like that wouldn't let you clean her bedpan."

Kevin wondered if Marty was obnoxious because he was a skeletal, awkward kid with a bad case of acne, who was picked on by just about every kid in the school except Kevin. Kevin told Marty to grow up.

"Think about it, fool. Gina's gonna let you do her homework. Then she's gonna thank you by having Billy beat the crap out of you."

"It's not your worry, Marty."

"Come to think of it, Kevin, I've never even seen you with a girl. What does that tell you about your chances with Gina?"

Kevin was about to head to class when Cheryl appeared in front of him. Standing in the same spot where Gina had stood, the tall, big-boned girl with a boyish face and short blond hair asked Kevin what Gina wanted.

"Help with her homework."

"And are you?"

"Gonna help her?" Kevin asked, surprised that Cheryl cared what he did.

"Well, are you?" she asked.

Even though he told Cheryl casually, "Yeah, I guess so," as though he hadn't given it much thought, there was no way he'd pass up a chance to be with Gina.

Of course, Marty couldn't let it go without putting in his

two cents. "Billy's gonna beat the crap out of Kevin when he finds out Gina's going to his house tonight."

"Perfect," Cheryl said, before walking away, leaving Kevin to wonder what she'd meant by it.

In an apparent fit of disbelief, Marty announced, "Oh my God, that girl's jealous," so loudly that some kids nearby looked at them.

Although Kevin told him, that besides being none of his business, it wasn't true, he knew from the stupid grin on Marty's face that Marty had more to say about it. Sure enough, Marty said, "Holy shit, you're doing Cheryl, aren't you?"

"Jesus, Marty, keep your voice down. Cheryl's in my French class. We talked a few times. That's all. So don't go starting any rumors."

Kevin knew that anyone foolish enough to confide in Marty opened themselves up to an incessant stream of questions about their private life, so when Marty asked him how he planned to pick up Gina without a car, Kevin ignored him.

Marty knew that Kevin's mother had deserted him and his dad. Marty didn't know that his dad had gone out of town on business again, leaving Kevin home alone, or that his dad had taken a cab to the airport, leaving his Mercedes in the garage so it wouldn't get dinged in the airport parking lot, or that the keys were hanging on the wall in the kitchen by the back door.

Marty pressed him for an answer. "Well?"

"What do you want, Marty?"

"For starters, the answers to the Bio homework."

After telling Marty, "Not happening," and, "I'll be late for calculous," Kevin turned his back on Marty and walked away.

Marty yelled, "When Billy's done with you, you'll look like roadkill."

* * * *

On her way to her locker to get the textbook for her English class Gina heard a deep threatening voice behind her ask, "What were you doing talking to that little twerp?"

She knew from the voice it was Billy but pretended she hadn't heard him. He grabbed her arm and yanked on it, forcing her to stop and turn around. She told him to let go and tried to pull her arm away.

He squeezed her arm harder, said, "You'd better stay away from him."

Now she'd have to wear long sleeves for the rest of the week to hide the bruise. "You can't tell me what to do."

"I just did," he said, then let go of her arm to reach for the top button of her blouse.

She brushed his hand away. He pushed her hard, against the lockers. She had to arch her back to avoid the locker handle digging into it.

When she told him, "I'm never going out with you," he grabbed her chin and forced her to look at him. "Don't make me hurt you."

He left, but not until she'd lied to him, promising to stay away from Kevin. She still planned to go to Kevin's house because she needed help with math if she was going to graduate. But now she had to worry about what Billy would do to Kevin and to her tomorrow when he found out she'd lied about not going to Kevin's house.

Walking on to her locker she spotted Mr. Taylor standing in the hallway monitoring the kids going to class. At least a head taller than any of the kids in the hallway he was hard to miss, and she'd have to walk right past him to get to her locker.

Knowing the guidance counselor was waiting for her because of the way he stared at her, Gina wondered what he wanted with her, wondered what she'd done wrong. Just before she passed him he called out her name. She stopped in the middle of the hall and waited for him to come to her, causing the mass of kids moving through the hallway to bunch up as they jostled with each other to get around her, like water flowing around a rock in a stream.

Leaning closer to her than necessary to be heard, Mr.

Taylor whispered in her ear as though they were conspirators. "I'll fix your math grade so you can graduate if you come to my office after school today and show me how grateful you are."

She shook her head, pretending she didn't understand.

Looming over her menacingly, he said, "Don't play innocent with me. I know you're screwing Billy," and, "If you don't show up I'll fix it so you never graduate."

She knew it wouldn't do any good to tell him she wasn't screwing Billy and that she never had, because it was all over school thanks to Billy lying about it to his buddies. Although she had no intention of going to Mr. Taylor's office after school, she told him she would just so he'd leave her alone.

She walked away thinking the day couldn't get any worse, but then spotted Mandy leaning on the locker next to hers. She couldn't stand the girl, but was civil to her because Gina's mother and Mandy's mother were good friends.

"So," Mandy said, affecting disgust, "I heard you're going to that weirdo's house tonight."

Gina told Mandy it was none of her business as she dropped the books she'd been carrying into the bottom of her locker.

Mandy gasped then said, "Oh my God, you really are. You're going to his house."

Mandy was the last person Gina wanted to talk to about it because Mandy couldn't keep a secret. She'd tell her boyfriend, Jared, who was Billy's best friend, Then Jared would tell Billy about it, and Billy would get especially mad because his friend would know Gina had made a fool of him. No telling what Billy would do then.

While Gina pretended to look for a book on the top shelf of her locker and hoped Mandy would leave, she thought about the night her mother had started pressuring her to go out with Billy; how her mother had heard from Mandy's mother that Billy was the school football star and interested in Gina, and how for weeks since then her mother and Billy's friends had been pressuring Gina to go out with him.

Slamming her locker door Gina told Mandy the same thing she'd told her mother. "I'm never going out with Billy."

Mandy closed her eyes, and hugging her books to her chest like a lovesick young girl, she leaned back against the lockers. "I'd let him do anything he wanted to me."

Gina stopped what she was doing to look at Mandy. "Are you serious?"

Mandy nodded her head.

Instead of saying, "You are such a slut," which is what she was thinking, Gina said, "You want him, he's yours" then left for class.

* * * *

Cheryl spotted Billy in the hallway up ahead and yelled to him. "Hey, Billy, wait up."

Billy stopped and looked around, scowling when he spotted her, the scowl changing to a leer as he watched her approach him, because struggling to force her way through the flow of kids had left her out of breath, and her chest was heaving. Billy made no effort to hide his interest. Cheryl would have scolded any other boy for doing that but liked the attention from Billy.

She started the conversation with the first of several lines she'd rehearsed. "I heard you threatened Kevin."

"So what?"

"Did you know Gina's going to his house tonight?"

Looking her in the eye for the first time he squinted at her warily. "What's it to you?"

She took his hand and held it against her leg just below the hem of her skirt. She didn't do it just because it felt good, which it did. She did it so he wouldn't leave after she told him the lie she knew would make him really angry. "Gina told Kevin she'd have sex with him if he helped her with her math."

Cheryl heard a low guttural sound as Billy's face turned a deep shade of red.

Pulling Billy's hand up under her skirt, Cheryl said, "You need a girl who appreciates a man."

For several moments she enjoyed Billy's hand stroking her thigh. Then he said what she'd been waiting to hear. "Come over to my house tonight?"

Saying, "I don't know," got the reaction she hoped for - a scowl. It was her cue to give him the demure look she'd perfected in front of the mirror the night before, and to tell him, "Okay, but I'll put up a hell of a fight if you try anything."

That turned his scowl into a grin, assuring her that she'd been right about Billy – that he liked a girl who made him work for it. She turned her back on him and walked away. That's when she smiled, and this time the smile was genuine, because the next time Billy forced himself on her it would be in his bed instead of just in her head.

* * * *

A short girl with a pixie haircut Gina didn't recognize, one who looked young enough to be a freshman, stopped Gina and pulled her aside "I saw you talking to my dad."

Gina had heard that Mr. Taylor had a daughter in school and thought she remembered that the girl's name was Donna. Gina didn't think anything good would come of talking to Donna, but when Gina started to walk away Donna threatened her. "You're giving me a ride to Billy's house tonight. If you don't, I'll tell my dad you're selling drugs to kids at school."

Gina spun around to confront her.

"You'll be expelled," Donna said.

"I'll tell your dad it's a lie."

Giving Gina a little evil-looking smile, Donna asked, "Who do you think he's gonna believe? You or his little angel?"

Gina imagined slapping Donna hard enough to knock the grin off her face, but it just wasn't something she could do. With her frustration at an all-time high Gina promised to make the arrangements with Billy.

"Pick me up at eight," Donna said, "and make sure it's just me and Billy, or I tell my dad."

As she watched Donna walk away Gina decided it was the worst day of her life.

* * * *

The first thing Kevin did when he got home from school was look up Gina's address. Then he sat in the kitchen to wait until seven-forty-five when he'd leave to pick her up. With nothing to do but watch the clock until then, he got his English Lit textbook out and tried reading ahead, but he couldn't concentrate. He warmed up the dinner his dad had left in the refrigerator for him but he couldn't eat it. He was so nervous about being with Gina, and so worried about facing Billy in the morning, that not even watching television helped.

At seven-forty-five he took the keys for his dad's Mercedes off the hook by the kitchen door, pressing the button on the garage door opener on his way into the garage. He got into the car and put the key in the ignition then took a deep breath before starting it.

Six minutes later, with his heart beating so fast and hard he felt feint, he brought the car to a stop in Gina's driveway. As she got into the car she flashed a big glad-to-see-you smile at him, and the smile looked so genuine Kevin wondered if Gina might actually like him.

Kevin put his hand on the gearshift then waited for her to close her door so he could put the car in reverse. But instead of closing her door she put her hand on his, the whisper-soft touch of her silky-smooth skin leading him to wonder if her lips were as soft as her hands and what it would be like to kiss them.

But then she said, "I need to tell you something about Billy before we go," and it dashed whatever hopes he'd had that their arrangement might lead to something more than just helping her with her homework.

She frowned deeply, causing little wrinkles to form by her

eyebrows. "Billy knows that I'm going to your house to study. I don't know who told him. It wasn't me. But he'll he crazy angry. So I won't blame you if you tell me to get out of the car."

Imagining Billy waiting for him on the school steps in the morning with a shit-eating grin on his face, Kevin felt a tingling in his bowls. He asked her if she was Billy's girlfriend.

Her answer, that, "I'd never go out with that creep," was good enough for him. He reached for the gear shift again.

She touched his hand again. "There's more. And it's gonna sound a little sound crazy."

Of course, what did he expect? Being with Gina was too good to be true. She told him about Donna's threat.

"Geeze," was all he could think to say. He stared at the steering wheel and tried to think of a solution for her problem, but his brain went blank.

"Kevin?"

Coming out of a stupor, he asked her, "That's Taylor's kid, isn't it?"

Gina grimaced and nodded her head.

"You should tell him what Donna said."

"I can't."

"Why not?"

She told him about Mr. Taylor's threat and that she hadn't gone to his office after school.

He stared at the steering wheel again.

"Now do you want me to get out of your car?"

Telling her to get out was the only sensible thing to do. She'd certainly given him enough reasons. But blame it on hormones, because if there was a chance, no matter how slim, that he might make a connection with this girl he was going to try. And he'd start by helping her with Donna and Mr. Taylor. He didn't know how, but he would.

Gina swung her legs out of the car.

He reached for her arm. "No, stay. We'll give Donna a ride."

The moment he stopped the car in the Taylor's driveway, a skinny girl with short blond hair and a young boy's body came

115

out wearing a skirt that looked much too short for a girl her age. Kevin remembered seeing her in school but hadn't known she was Taylor's daughter. He backed out of the Taylors' driveway as soon as Donna got in the car.

* * * *

Billy was at home sitting on a stool at the kitchen counter looking up Cheryl's number in the phonebook when his mother came into the room dressed in a working-man's shirt and slacks. Billy hated having a factory worker for a mother. She once told his friends the look was called "factory-chic" then laughed out loud, which just made his embarrassment worse. He wondered what the hell his dad had ever seen in her.

When she told Billy to take the dog out for a walk, he pretended he hadn't heard her.

She kicked his stool, said, "Hey, I'm talking to you."

He'd just found Cheryl's phone number and was trying to save it in his cell phone when she yanked on his arm. He was so startled he dropped the phone. As it clattered on the floor she held the dog's leash out toward him and said, "I'll pay you."

Billy muttered, "Damn right you will," as he picked up his phone.

He snatched the leash from his mother and called the dog. A big Lab bounded into the room and jumped up on him, putting its paws on his chest. Billy twisted his head to the side and shoved the dog away to avoid its slobbering mouth. It came back at him, panting and flinging drool and wagging its tail as he struggled to hook the leash on its collar.

At the snap of the leash it lunged toward the sliding glass doors that opened to the back yard. Billy jerked on the leash so hard the dog wheezed. When he opened the door the dog lunged again. Billy jerked on its collar again. The dog coughed and gagged and pulled Billy outside.

As his mother closed the door behind them she yelled, "And I don't want you bringing any girls here while I'm at work."

He imagined having Cheryl pinned on the bed under him, and while he thought about that and tried to untangle the leash wrapped around his legs, he heard a door slam at his neighbor's house and turned to look.

The woman who lived there strutted across her back deck toward Billy in a bathrobe and curlers, yelling, "Don't you dare let that dog crap in my flowers."

Then she reached up to fuss with her hair, the motion pulling her untied bathrobe open, giving Billy an intimate view of her overweight, middle-aged body. He made a show of bending over and pretending to wretch. She swore at him then went back inside, her cat shooting out of the house when she opened the door.

He didn't care about the cat, except that it was her cat. He watched it strut off the deck into his yard as though it owned the place. Billy let go of his dog's leash then bent down and pointed its face at the cat, holding it there until the dog jerked its head so he was sure the Lab had spotted it.

The dog barked. The cat took off at a dead run. The dog surged after it trailing its leash. The cat darted under a hedgerow at the property line. The Lab, unable to squeeze through the bushes whimpered and paced and barked. A moment later Billy heard the squeal of car tires and smiled at the possibilities.

After dragging the Lab back in the house, Billy walked around the block to check on the sound. Sure enough, the crazy neighbor's cat had been hit by a car. He carefully picked the remains up by its tail and carried it to the neighbor's house and threw it on her deck where she'd be sure to see it.

He wished he could wait around to enjoy the woman's face when she found her cat, but he didn't want to miss Cheryl if she came early. Back inside, Billy looked through the cupboards for a drink to celebrate the death of his neighbor's cat while he waited for Cheryl. One glass of whiskey later the doorbell rang.

He half-hoped it was the crazy woman from next door coming to bitch about her dead cat. He definitely hadn't expected to see Mandy standing at the door, especially in an extra-low-cut tank top and very short skirt. He definitely liked what he saw but figured she probably just wanted to talk to him about some stupid girl problem, the absolute last thing he wanted to do. He told her he didn't have time and started to close the door.

"I heard about Gina going to Kevin's," she said, blocking the door with her foot.

Billy did not want to talk to about that, especially with Mandy who'd blab about it to Jared. "So?"

"So, I could make you forget about her."

He wondered if she meant what he thought she meant, wondered if he could be that lucky. "Oh yeah, and how are you gonna do that?"

"I'm not gonna do it out here, am I?" Mandy said, rubbing her hand on his crotch.

Feeling himself get hard, Billy stepped back to let Mandy in, giving her a thorough once-over as she walked past him. Then he remembered that Cheryl would be there soon. After a moment of angst an idea came to him, the best idea he'd had in a very long time. If Cheryl showed up while he was doing Mandy, he'd make it a threesome. He couldn't have planned things better.

* * * *

On the way to Billy's house Gina thought about Donna and what Billy might do to her, and as much as she liked the idea of Billy teaching Donna a lesson, Gina didn't want to be responsible for Donna losing her virginity. So she told Kevin to turn right at the next corner. Half a block later she told him to stop the car.

Trying her best to sound sincere Gina pointed at a puke-green, two-story house across the street. "The green one's Billy's."

After fussing with her hair and the collar on her blouse Donna said, "Well?"

Gina was tempted to tell her the truth, that Billy wouldn't even notice her clothes. He'd just rip them off. Instead she told Donna, "He won't be able to keep his hands off of you," which got a smile from her.

As soon as Donna was out of the car Gina told Kevin to go, "and hurry."

He turned left at the next corner then pulled over to the curb and asked, "What now?"

"I wanted to be long gone when someone answered the door and told her that nobody named Billy lived there."

"That was the wrong house?"

"Yep."

"Why do that?"

"If that girl's a virgin now, she won't be when Billy gets done with her. I don't need that on my conscience."

"But she'll tell her dad you're selling drugs?"

"Nothing I can do about that."

Kevin felt an urgent desire to help Gina. He closed his eyes, tried to concentrate.

"Hey," Gina said, "where'd you go?"

In the twenty seconds or so that he'd had his eyes closed he'd had an idea. Not a perfect one. It wouldn't make Gina's problems go away, but he liked it anyway, and watched closely for her reaction. "We could have some fun with this?"

Tipping her pretty head she squinted at him. "How?"

"We'll teach Mr. Taylor a lesson?"

"How?"

"Call him. Tell him that Donna's at Billy house."

As her frown morphed into a smile she gave his hand a pat and said, "Clever boy."

Then she took out her cell phone, and with the phone on speaker, told Mr. Taylor, "Your daughter's at Billy's. They're up in his bedroom doing things your wife won't do with you."

Taylor only got as far as saying, "Who the …," before Gina ended the call.

"Nice one," Kevin said. "If that doesn't make him crazy

119

nothing will."

"Yeah, well I can kiss my diploma good-bye."

Kevin apologized for suggesting she call Mr. Taylor. She told him not to worry. He couldn't help but worry.

"You know what I wish, Kevin?"

"What?"

"I wish I could be there when Taylor storms into Billy's room. I mean, as long as I'm gonna pay for it anyway, I should get to enjoy it."

"Then let's."

"How are we gonna get into Billy's bedroom?"

"If Taylor does go to Billy's house, the trouble's gonna start as soon as Billy opens the front door. We'll hide outside and watch."

This time when Gina smiled, instead of just glancing at him and flashing a quick smile, she made and held eye contact with him long enough to make him feel self-conscious. And after saying, "I love it," she looked at him funny. Maybe she was starting to like him. He could hope, couldn't he?

* * * *

Kevin parked two doors past Billy's house so Billy wouldn't see their car. They crossed a neighbor's lawn and cut through a hedgerow, approaching Billy's house from the side so he'd be less likely to see them. When they got within twenty feet of the house Kevin heard what he assumed was a female having an orgasm, the sounds coming from an open upstairs window.

Gina whispered, "Happy girl."

Kevin looked away - he knew he'd turn red as a ripe tomato if he made eye contact with Gina while some girl was making sexually explicit noises. They hid behind the overgrown yew bushes in front of Billy's house.

It wasn't long before a small, white pickup truck spotted with rust turned into Billy's driveway and skidded to a halt. Mr. and Mrs. Taylor got out, both of them, dressed in suburban-casual shorts and tees. Both of them took big quick strides toward Billy's front door.

About halfway there, a shriek from the girl upstairs got their attention, their heads snapping around to look up at the window. Mr. Taylor stepped back from the house to get a better look. Then, running to the front door, he tried the doorknob. Mrs. Taylor rang the bell, but didn't wait for anyone to answer before beating on the door.

Pushing her aside Mr. Taylor pounded on the door much harder than his wife had, his hammering becoming ever more frantic as the seconds ticked by. Kevin wondered if the door was a substitute for Billy's face, or if Mr. Taylor was trying to drown out the noises coming from upstairs, but even after the X rated racket stopped, Mr. Taylor went on pounding like a madman.

A minute or two later Billy opened the door. Mr. Taylor shoved a stunned-looking Billy out of the way, rushing past him into the house. Billy grabbed Taylor from behind by the collar as he went by, yanking him backwards so hard that Taylor's feet shot out in front of him and he went down, hitting his head on the corner of a hall table on his way to meet the floor.

When Mrs. Taylor tried to get past Billy to help her husband, Billy stiff-armed her, driving her back outside with a hand to her chest. Then Billy grabbed Mr. Taylor under the armpits, pulling him up onto his feet, making it look as easy as picking up a stuffed doll.

Mr. Taylor teetered in the doorway until Billy put his foot against Taylor's back and shoved him out. Mr. Tylor stumbled ten feet or so into the yard before landing face down in the grass.

Grinning mightily, Billy stepped outside and yelled, "Loser."

Mr. Taylor rolled over and sat up holding his head. Blood trickled out from under his left hand where his head had hit the table. After trying unsuccessfully to stand up, he ended up on all fours in the grass, which earned him a laugh from Billy. Mrs. Taylor gave Billy a dirty look then went over to help her husband.

Just then a big black Lab ran out of the house in a frenzy of barking and tail wagging. It went straight for Mr. Taylor, almost knocking him to the ground again. Mrs. Taylor pulled on the dog's collar to keep it at bay while her husband struggled to his feet.

Kevin stepped out of the bushes then with Gina right behind him.

When Billy spotted them he said, "What the hell?"

By then Mr. Taylor had managed to stand up, and had no sooner gotten to his feet than he stumbled toward Billy, lunging at him when he got within a few feet of him. Billy stepped aside, easily avoiding Mr. Taylor who lost his balance making a wild grab for Billy.

Mr. Taylor had regained his footing again and looked as though he was preparing for another assault when Mandy appeared at the door. Looking disheveled and confused, and wearing nothing but a large tee shirt that said, "Sex with me will set you free," she asked Billy, "What the hell's going on?"

A confused looking Mr. Taylor demanded, "Where's my daughter?"

Kevin thought the surprised look on Billy's face when he said, "How the hell should I know?" looked genuine.

Mandy told Mr. Taylor, "Well she sure as hell isn't here."

The Taylors looked at each other. Billy told them they'd been had.

Putting her arm around her husband Mrs. Taylor said to him, "I told you Donna wouldn't have anything to do with the likes of him."

Mr. Taylor started to object. She cut him off, said, "Let's get you home so I can put something on that cut" then led him toward their truck.

Mandy shouted, "Hey, Mrs. Taylor."

Mrs. Taylor stopped and looked back at her, glowering.

"You want to know the truth about your lecher of a husband?"

Mrs. Taylor asked Mandy what she meant. Mr. Taylor told Mandy she was making a big mistake.

Mandy ignored the threat. "I got sent to your husband for detention twice this year, and both times he told me I wouldn't get a mark on my record if I had sex with him."

Mrs. Taylor gasped, said, "He wouldn't" then started shaking her head.

A smiling Mandy nodded her head, told Mrs. Taylor. "Well he did. And we did."

Mrs. Taylor looked at her husband as though she had a question for him. But if she did, she didn't put it into words. Kevin wondered if she already knew what his answer would be and didn't want to hear him say it, because that would make it real.

Billy began chanting, "Taylor is a pervert."

After calling Mandy a liar, Mr. Taylor yelled at Billy to shut up.

Mandy told Mrs. Taylor, "Go ahead, ask around. I'm not the only girl at school he screwed."

Knowing that Mr. Taylor would lose his job, Kevin was ready to leave because that solved Gina's problems with both Mr. Taylor and his daughter. But he heard a door slam and looked for the source.

A chubby, middle-aged woman with a tangled mass of bright-red hair hanging down to her waist was marching toward them from the house next door wearing a shapeless flower-print dress that stopped just above her hiking boots.

When she got within ten feet of Billy she shrieked, "You killed my cat, you bastard." When she got within five feet of Billy she pointed a gun at him.

Billy, who didn't seem to be the least bit afraid of the woman or the gun, shrugged his shoulders. "Nobody gives a shit about your stupid cat."

The woman walked over to Billy's Lab and held the gun to its head. "We'll see how you like it when I kill your dog."

The Lab nudged the gun then tried to lick the woman's hand. Distracted by the dog she didn't see Billy dive for her. He dropped her like a tackle dummy, driving her to the ground, hard. Standing effortlessly, he towered over the woman. She was much slower to recover, had just gotten up on her hands and knees when Billy shoved her with his foot, sending her sprawling in the grass.

Scooping up the gun she'd dropped, he pointed it at her. "Your turn, bitch."

Then he seemed to have second thoughts, standing still for several moments before spinning around to point the gun at Gina. "This is all your fault. If you'd given me what I wanted, none of this would've happened."

Without thinking, Kevin stepped to the left between the gun and Gina, realizing too late that he'd bet his life on Billy being reasonable. As he looked down the barrel of the gun the extent of the danger sunk in. Billy had just been in two scrapes, one with Mr. Taylor, and another with his crazy neighbor, and the scuffles would have gotten Billy's testosterone raging, making it more likely he'd do something foolish, like shooting Kevin.

It didn't help that Billy was grinning like a madman when he took a step closer and poked Kevin in the stomach with the gun. "You know what I'm gonna do to you, punk?

Answering seemed pointless. He just hoped his knees wouldn't give out.

Billy grinned, said, "I'm gonna put a hole in you."

For years after that Kevin wondered what would've happened if the police hadn't showed up then, their car screeching to a stop in Billy's driveway.

Billy looked down at the gun in his hand then looked at the two policemen getting out of the patrol car. He let the hand holding the gun fall to his side.

One policemen, a heavy-set man in a rumpled uniform who needed a shave, looked old enough to retire but not healthy enough to chase bad guys. The other one had a crewcut and walked kind of funny, as though his uniform was uncomfortable. Kevin thought he looked healthy enough to chase bad guys but not old enough.

The woman from next-door shouted at them. "Where the hell have you been? I called twenty minutes ago."

Ignoring her, the older cop walked over to Billy and held his hand out demanding the gun. Billy, who looked disgusted, as though something terribly unfair had happened to him, handed it over.

Pointing at Billy the neighbor woman told the young cop, "That pervert killed my cat."

Mr. Taylor pointed at Billy. "Forget the god-damned cat. Someone told us our under-age daughter was here screwing that asshole."

The policeman told them to shut up. The crazy woman from next door stepped in front of him, her face just inches from his, and put her hands on her hips. She asked him what he was going to do about her cat.

He said, "Jesus, lady, give it a rest. It's only a cat."

Shaking her head, she mumbled something that sounded to Kevin like an obscenity before walking back toward her house.

Billy yelled something unpleasant at the woman as the older cop pushed him into the cruiser. The young cop joined his partner there for a short discussion, after which he took a pad of paper out of their car and said, "Nobody leaves until I have a statement from every one of you."

Kevin sat down on Billy's front steps. Gina sat next to him and gave his hand a gentle squeeze. "You really are a decent guy."

He asked her if she still wanted help with math.

"Yeah, I do, but I already learned something from you."

He looked at the people around them. "That they're all nuts?"

"No silly. The worst day of your life will end up being the best day of your life if you meet someone special."

ZIT HAULERS

From my seat in a booth by the window of Morey's Diner I watched a woman and young boy walk out to their car. The boy's attention was so intensely focused on the thing in his hands that he drifted away from her, heading right for our truck and the murderous cargo under our tarpaulin.

My boss, Orlando Sacco, had parked our truck out beyond the reach of the parking lot lights where he hoped no one would notice it or hear the growling of the dead things under the tarp. I watched the boy, who couldn't have been more than ten years old, stop to look at it with his head tipped a little to the right.

I wanted to beat on the window, wanted to scream, "Jesus, kid, get the hell away from there," but I knew he wouldn't hear me, so I held my breath and watched.

As the woman walked on, obviously unaware the boy was no longer with her, the stupid kid looked around furtively, the way kids do before they do something they know they shouldn't. I knew then that I had to go save his sorry little ass.

Eating like a sailor who'd been marooned on a deserted island and left to starve, Orlando was oblivious to the drama unfolding outside. Before running for the door, I whispered to him, "Goddamn kid's headed straight for our truck."

"Whatever you do," he said, grabbing my wrist, "do not make a scene. If someone complains and I lose my contract you're out of a job."

I tried to appear casual as I walked through the diner on my way outside. I should've been running. If not for Orlando's warning I would've been, because discrete could get the dumb kid killed.

I yelled, "Hey kid," the instant I stepped outside.

He ignored me, but not our load of zombies in transit, or ZITs as we like to call them. The loud snarling reaction my voice got from them would have been enough to scare away any sane adult, but this was a boy and boys throw stones at wasp nests.

The woman had heard me yell and turned around. She looked at me then toward our truck. She must've heard the ZITs because she made a face, looking confused at first then frightened. I think she remembered her kid then because she looked around frantically.

By then the kid was within a couple feet of our truck. She gasped when a boney arm shot out from under the tarp and tried to grab him. Obviously ignorant and extraordinarily stupid, the kid played a deadly game - slapping the ZIT's hand away. I broke into a run.

The woman screamed, "Get away from there, Joey."

The kid glanced at the woman then at me. Already running, I'd have my hands on him in seconds, but he must have been dying to know what was under the tarp because the suicidal little fool lifted the corner of it. Those ZITs that still had a viable optical nerve went berserk, which prompted the rest of them to sniff the air or turn a decomposed ear toward the commotion, depending on which senses they had left. Pretty soon all of them had gone berserk and the truck was swaying from the violence of their struggle to get at the fresh meat nearby.

And that's when everything went to crap. One of the ZITs fell out of the truck. When they're riled they'll climb on top of each other like army ants. I guess the pile got high enough for one of them to fall over the side. Its body landed like a sack of loose bones. Its head bounced on the pavement like a bowling ball.

I heard a woman scream behind me and looked around. Orlando was coming out of the diner along with five other patrons. I would've yelled to him to hurry but the kid screamed then. Maybe he'd heard the woman scream and turned his back on the ZIT to look. Anyway, it had grabbed him just before I did. When I tried to pull the ZIT's hand off the kid's arm, I got a handful of mushy, rotted flesh.

I yelled, "A little help here, Orlando," but when I looked back he was holding the kid's mother, pretending to comfort her. So, apparently saving the kid was my problem.

I used both hands to twist and bend the ZIT's wrist back until the bone broke with an audible crack. Its hand dangled from its arm by a single stubborn tendon. I pulled the fingers on the thing's other hand off the kid one at a time, snapping them like dead twigs while it tried to sink some scary-looking teeth fragments in me.

I saw a blur to my left, felt something brush my shirtsleeve then heard bone shatter. The ZIT slumped to the pavement.

Having smashed its head in with a tire iron Orlando told me, "Throw the carcass in the cab, we'll ditch it later."

After dragging it to the passenger door by one of its emaciated legs I bent it over and held its head between its knees and dropped my weight on its shoulders. Its spine broke on the second try. I bent it into thirds and stuffed it into the cab on the floor of the passenger side so it wouldn't be in Orlando's way while he was driving.

Then I picked up the fragments of crushed ZIT skull and the finger bones I'd broken off, tossing the rubbish in the cab. By then the kid was sobbing pathetically and Orlando was holding his mother again, which made the boy my problem again.

I told him, "You're okay, kid," even though I knew he wasn't because I'd noticed a spot of fresh blood on his arm.

It had to be the kid's blood, probably from a bite. I wiped

it away with my shirtsleeve before his mother saw it and blamed me for letting it happen. If it was a bite she'd find out soon enough. There wasn't anything anyone could do for a bite.

Meanwhile, the truck was still swaying like a ship in a storm, the ZITs sounded like wolves fighting over a fresh kill, and a bunch of people had come out of the diner to watch the show. So much for Orlando's warning about calling attention to our cargo.

Orlando brought the woman over to get her kid. Without taking her eyes off of our truck she asked him, "What the hell is in there?"

He told her to take the kid home then told me, "Time for us to get the hell outta here?"

Back on the road, headed west into the darkness again, I asked him why he hadn't helped me with the kid.

"That woman needed a hug."

I told him I didn't think so.

"You are mistaken," he said. "She was in great need of reassurance, and sadly, you are no good at comforting women."

Orlando was right – when it came to women I never knew what to say or do, but otherwise he was full of shit and I told him so.

He grinning at me like a fool, he slapped me on the back, said, "You have seen right through me, amigo. I am the one who wanted the hug. But you got to play the hero and for that you should be happy."

I told him the ZIT had bitten the kid. That shut him up for a while.

I had trouble getting comfortable with the ZIT's carcass under my feet. Even with it folded in thirds my knees were up near my chin. And right behind our seat, just inches from my head, there was a small window that looked into the back of the truck. The ZITs were right up against the glass, clawing at the window. Even though I'd made the trip to the lab a dozen times before, I still found their relentless desire to chew on me unsettling. Orlando on the other hand, seemed oblivious to the ungodly racket.

I asked him, "Doesn't that ever get to you?"

For a ZIT hauler, Orlando wasn't very big, but he had a lot of attitude, and he was fast and tough, and everything I knew about tracking and wrangling ZITs I'd learned from him. The same scarred, rugged-looking face that had held him back before the onslaught had served him well in the dangerous times since then. You can say what you like about everyone having an equal chance in life, but people who look the part they play have less to prove, and success is more likely to be their friend.

Orlando shrugged his shoulders. "It's no different than having cattle back there."

I was reminding him that, "Cattle don't try to eat you," when the CB radio crackled to life with a call from the agency that contracted with Orlando to transport ZITs.

After he had acknowledged the call, Thelma, the agency's dispatcher, told us, "We got word that protesters are planning to hijack one of our trucks tonight. There's even talk of them turning the ZITs loose."

Before signing off Orlando assured her we'd be careful. It was a lie - worrying wasn't his style. He changed the radio station to one playing an old punk rock song. I needed a distraction too but his music choice grated on my nerves. Even though Orlando often ignored me when I talked, talking helped keep me sane, or as near to sane as one could be these days. So I talked. "You know what's weird?"

"You are, my very gloomy friend."

"Even though those things are so driven by their craving for living flesh they're almost impossible to stop, they don't ever fight each other for it."

Orlando took his eyes off the road long enough to look at me askance. "I am in awe of where your mind takes you."

"I'm not saying there's anything like cooperation among

those things, but humans routinely kill each other for less."

"You may have a point."

I asked him if he was just humoring me.

Affecting a Spanish accent he said, "I would not do that, señor," but he was grinning.

To keep my mind off our cargo and the warning about the protestors I counted the abandoned houses we passed on the desolate country road rolling under the truck. I didn't blame people for moving into town. With zombies still on the prowl, the country was a scary place at night. Even if you could get the authorities to respond to your 911 call, by the time they showed up it might be too late for you and yours.

I needed one more abandoned house to make fifteen when I saw someone walking on the side of the road up in the distance, out at the limit of the truck's headlights. No one in their right mind walked a country road alone at night. As we got closer our lights revealed a woman, assuming the woman's clothes actually had a woman in them. You couldn't be sure what was what wearing anymore.

Orlando backed off the gas. I knew he was waiting to get a good look at her before he made up his mind whether or not to stop. Immediately after we shot passed her Orlando swerved onto the shoulder of the road. As the truck slid to a stop in the dirt, I heard the ZITs slamming against the wall of the cab behind us.

The first thing I did when I got out of the truck was throw the ZIT that had been on the floor beneath my feet into the brush. Then I stood on the side of the road with Orlando to wait for the stranger. She held up a hand to shade her eyes when he shone a flashlight on her.

Wearing a low-cut tank top and a skirt covering a mere fraction of her thighs she was an unlikely sight on a dark, lonely, country road. Stopping near the back of the truck she eyed it warily.

Orlando yelled to her over the growling of the ZITs. "Kinda dangerous hitchhiking after dark, don't you think?"

She came a little closer, but tentatively, like a shy dog approaching a stranger holding a dog treat. In the glare of Orlando's flashlight I saw that she had makeup on, like the girls I remembered from the sweet days before the epidemic. I'd forgotten how good a little well-applied face paint looked. She took the cap off her head and shook out her hair. A lovey brown cascade fell to her shoulders and settled around her face. You can usually find something that's not quite right about everyone's face, but I couldn't find anything about hers that wasn't perfect. But she looked spooked, and who could blame her with a couple dozen ZITs worked into in a raucous frenzy.

"Jesus," she said, "what the hell's in there?"

Orlando told her not to worry, that she'd be safe with him, but dressed like she was Orlando would be more of a threat to her than the ZITs.

Smiling at Orlando she asked, "You offering me a ride?"

I told her we weren't allowed to pick up hitchhikers. Orlando told her to ignore me.

She held her hand out to him. "Name's Margot."

He winked at her, said, "Orlando" holding her hand a little longer than necessary. She smiled at him coquettishly.

I was about to introduce myself when Orlando slapped me on the shoulder and smiled at me like a long lost friend. "What say we get these pigs to market?"

Then he walked around behind the truck toward the driver's side. Margot watched him until he was out of sight. Checking out his ass no doubt. I held the passenger door open for her. She climbed up into the cab, showing pretty much everything in the process. She caught me looking and smiled, but it wasn't the same "anything you want" smile she'd flashed at Orlando.

She frowned when she realized her head would be just inches from the dead things clawing at the window behind us. She stared at them. I told her they were like druggies.

"Druggies?" she said, looking at me as though I was nuts.

"Really?"

"They're addicted to human flesh, and like drug addicts they'll do anything to satisfy their cravings. Of course, in some ways they're also like religions extremists because you can't reason with them and you can't appease them."

After giving me a pained look she looked at Orlando, gently putting her hand on his arm then asking him, "Do they bother you?"

"Are you kidding?" he said, with a big shit-eating grin. "Where am I gonna find so many women who want to eat me?"

It was typical Orlando, but instead of getting upset she asked him, "What are you guys?"

Orlando, who thought of himself as the epitome of the rugged American individual, like Gary Cooper in the movie "High Noon," told her he was an independent hunter-hauler, and that, "I contract with an outfit that supplies government labs with The Dead."

"That's what they call them?" she asked, "The Dead?"

I told her that the government lab rats referred to the syndrome as a "disease enabled afterlife disorder."

Orlando told her that spelled "Dead," as if she couldn't figure it out for herself. She looked pretty, not stupid.

After a moment of silence, during which she frowned and looked at her feet, she asked Orlando if we were part of some illegal government plot.

"What makes you think that?"

"Why else would you travel at night?"

He nodded his head at the window behind us. "The ZITs upset people. We get a lot of complaints if we travel during the day, but those same people are hunkered down indoors at night."

"Did you just call them ZITs?"

I told her it meant, "Zombies in transit."

She shook her head. Two abandoned houses later Orlando asked her where she was headed.

"Someplace with jobs."

He asked her where she was from.

"A place with no jobs."

He looked at Margot as though he didn't quite know what to make of her. "You're not much of a talker, are you?"

"I thought guys didn't like talkers."

After a few more miles had passed by under the truck Orlando asked her, "What do you call a naughty zombie?"

She shrugged her shoulders.

"Bad to the bone."

It wasn't much of a joke but the two of them laughed like fools, which told me it wasn't about the joke.

When the laughing died down Margot asked him, "How far you going?"

He told her we were headed for Binghamton, that the government had a big lab complex there.

"And what do they do with them?"

"Sweetheart," he said, "they pay me for as many of those things as I can deliver. And as long as they pay me, I don't care what they do to them."

A few miles later Orlando asked her, "What do you call it when a human gets into a bathtub with a zombie?"

"Oh, I know that one," she said, "a blood bath," and they laughed again.

After a while she asked him, "What happens if they get out?"

He reached in front of her to open the glove box, grinning at her as he brushed his arm against her chest unnecessarily. I have no doubt she would've slapped me for that but she smiled at Orlando. He took an automatic pistol out and held it up to show her. She asked him if it was loaded.

His answer, both typical and predictable, was. "Mine's always loaded because you never know when you're gonna meet a pretty girl."

She smiled at him then looked at me. Her attention lingered on my chest. I checked for a food stain.

She asked me, "Why the badge?"

But I didn't get to answer because Orlando held the plastic-coated photo ID hanging from the lariat around his neck close to her face and said, "Check out the good-looking guy in the picture."

"Yeah, nice mug," she said, "but why the badge?"

I told her you had to be licensed to haul ZITs, and that, "When the government figured out that taxes wouldn't make people nearly as mad if they called them fees they began charging fees for everything, even ZIT hauling licenses."

While I was talking Orlando had put his hand on Margot's thigh. She not only let him get away with it, she put her hand high up on the inside of his leg. Seeing her do that drove me nuts. I could only imagine what it was doing to Orlando.

While the two of them were busy fondling each other, the CB Radio crackled to life with another warning from Thelma. "Our spies tell us that you're the target tonight."

Orlando thanked her then signed off. I asked him if we were going to take a different route.

He waved his arm, as though brushing the threat aside. "I can't believe people actually get mad about the government experimenting on those things."

When I told him I could kinda see their point he said, "I didn't take you for a ZIT hugger."

I asked him if he had ever wondered about people in comas.

"You do know about that whole lack of oxygen to the brain causing irreparable damage thing."

When I told him, "Maybe that doesn't apply to ZITs," he told me I was nuts. Margot told me I had issues.

Several more abandoned houses later, Margot asked me if I had somebody waiting for me at home.

When I admitted that I did, she grinned at me and asked, "And how's the sex?"

"Really?" I said. "That's the first thing you ask about?"

She told me I was a stiff.

"You don't know anything about us. You've never even met my girlfriend."

She nudged me with her elbow. "Get it? I said you were a stiff."

I told her there was something wrong with her. It didn't stop her from asking me another equally inappropriate question. "So is she the passive type?"

I told her it was none of her business, but like Orlando she didn't seem to have any boundaries and wouldn't let it go. "Well, is she or isn't she?"

"Why would you ask me something like that?"

"I was just wondering if she was dead in bed."

Orlando laughed and told her, "Good one."

I asked her if we could talk about something else.

She said there wasn't anything else.

That was all the invitation Orlando needed for another grab-and-feel session. After a few minutes with his hand up Margot's skirt Orlando announced, "I gotta take a leak," then pulled the truck over and brought it to a shuddering stop.

I suspected he and Margot were up to something, and sure enough, Margot said, "Me too" then reached in the glove box for the automatic. "But I'm bringing this in case I run into a ZIT out there."

With the truck running and the headlights on I watched them disappear in the bushes. They weren't together but I figured they soon would be. As long as the truck was stopped I decided I might as well relieve myself, but to avoid them I wandered into the bushes behind the truck and was accordingly preoccupied when I heard Orlando's automatic. Stopping mid-stream I hurried back to the truck to see what had happened.

When I came out of the bushes Margot was waiting for me. With Orlando's gun pointed at me she told me, "Hands where I can see them, bozo."

When I asked her where Orlando was she nodded at the truck, told me, "Let 'em out."

"What the hell's wrong with you?"

"My brother's in there."

I couldn't believe I hadn't made the connection. It explained why a woman would be walking alone on a deserted country road at night. "Jesus, you're the one Thelma warned us about."

"Not much smarter than your cargo, are you?"

I started to say something. She told me to shut up.

But I couldn't. I was too scared to just stand there quietly and wait to be shot. "You think the government's working on a cure, that they'll be able to save your brother someday. But that's just what they tell people so they can go on doing the evil stuff they do at those labs."

She threatened to shoot me if I didn't let the ZITs out. After several delays on my part and increasingly convincing threats on her part, I released the tailgate latch. It swung down and hit the truck chassis with a loud clang, setting off the ZITs, like kicking a nest of hornets.

The moment I opened the gate the ZITs burst out in a frenzied hoard. I scrambled to get away. Moments later Margot screamed. I looked back. Several of the ZITs were on her. Waving the gun wildly and firing indiscriminately, none of her shots hit the things gnawing on her.

I backed up to avoid being shot and backed right into a ZIT. I twisted, hitting its head with my elbow as I spun around. But the damn thing grabbed my arm and bit me. I ripped its lower jaw off and shoved it away then fought my way into the cab of the truck.

I turned on the CB to put out a Mayday call. But as the radio crackled to life I realized that would be pointless. There wasn't anything anyone could do for me so I slumped down on the seat to await my fate. My one regret was not having the gun so I could blow my brains out, because the idea that I might soon be trapped with my thoughts inside a comatose-like dead body made me feel claustrophobic. Then I remembered the ZIT lab and wondered what they would do to me.

* * * *

Kevin had spent two hours helping his boss round up the ZITs that had mysteriously gotten away from one of the other contract haulers. They were wrangling the last one onto their truck. They'd found it trapped in the cab of the other hauler's truck. As ZITs go, it hadn't put up much of a fight.

Kevin climbed up and stood in the open passenger doorway of their truck where the ZITs could see him. He climbed into the truck box, moving slowly to entice the ZITs to follow him then climbed up and over the side before they could reach him. When they had jammed up against the cab in a frenzy to get at him, his partner, Marty, shoved the last ZIT through the gate then threw the latch and put the tailgate up. The one they'd taken from the cab of the truck didn't join the others trying to get a piece of him. It just stood there and stared at him.

And Kevin stared back at it until Marty yelled, "Let's go, Kevin. The sooner we get these ZITs to the lab the sooner we can go home."

After Kevin had settled into the passenger seat Marty asked him, "What the hell's bothering you?"

"That last one, the one we found in the cab of the truck, he was wearing a hauler badge."

"Yeah," Marty said, "he was one of the guys transporting this bunch, and now he's one of them. And if you don't get your mind back on the job it'll happen to you."

As a shiver worked its way up through Kevin's back and shoulders he told Marty, "That one gives me the creeps.

"Creepier than the usual 'I want to eat your organs' look?"

Kevin let the remark go and they rode in silence, but only for a few miles because something about the ZIT was still bothering him. "Marty?"

"Yeah?"

"You know the dogs with the human expressions, the ones that look like they're deep in thought?"

"You mean Russian Wolfhounds? What about 'em?"

"That ZIT had one of those looks, like it wanted to tell me something."

Marty told him he was spooked because of what had happened to the other haulers.

Marty was right about Kevin being spooked, but wrong about why. "It hardly even put up a fight. What about that?"

"Its heart wasn't in it."

When Kevin didn't say anything Marty backhanded his arm. "Get it? Its heart wasn't in it."

"Go ahead and laugh, Marty, but it was scared and it wanted to tell me something, I'm sure of it."

Kevin was saying, "You're nuts," when he spotted someone walking on the side of the road up in the distance, out at the limit of the truck's headlights.

KILLER LESSON

"**D**on't you let him die easy," was the first thing Christie said when she met Nick for the first time.

She didn't think the little man with the bad complexion and dull gray eyes wearing ill-fitting, outdated clothes looked the way a professional killer ought to look.

And when he said, "I can see from your expression that you're disappointed," his gravelly voice grated on her nerves.

"You think," he said, squinting at her, "that I'm less of a person than you, and yet you're gonna pay me to kill your husband. How do you reconcile that?"

Christie changed the subject because the last thing she wanted to do was argue morals with a reprobate. "My husband should be at her place by eight."

"Show me the money," Nick said, "before we go any further."

Christie had picked the place for their meeting, a crummy little working-man's bar, the kind you see in almost every inner-city neighborhood, the kind frequented by a few die-hard regulars; hard luck cases who wouldn't give her more than a passing glance. When she'd called to set up the meeting, Nick had told her to look for a guy sitting alone in a booth on the far side of the room where the lighting was poor, and that there'd be two drinks on the table.

She took an envelope out of her purse and handed it to the seedy-looking man sitting across from her. He opened it and flipped through the bills. He'd insisted that she pay him in used twenties. It made for a big stack of bills, and now, watching the low-life question her integrity by counting the money, it made her angry. She normally wouldn't have let someone like Nick get away with that, but she was glad to be rid of the money because giving him the money sealed her husband's fate.

Nick put the envelope in his coat pocket then pushed one of the drinks toward her. But a picture formed in her mind of the last person to drink from the glass and she said, "I don't think so," as she pushed it back across the table.

"Not very friendly, are we?" he said, grinning at her.

Appalled at him for thinking she'd befriend someone of his ilk, Christie tried to think of a response that would put him in his place.

While she struggled with that Nick said, "Your husband must have done something pretty bad."

The comment reminded Christie of a night two weeks earlier when Bobby, her devoted pain-in-the-ass little brother, had stopped by her place to tell her that her husband Chad was seeing one of Bobby's friends.

Everything about Bobby irritated her: the preppy beard, the thin line of dark stubble running along his weak chin, and the same close-set beady eyes she remembered from when he was a whiny little kid. She wasn't sure which she hated more, the message or the messenger.

"Well?" Nick said, startling her, "what about it?"

Christie told him, "My husband called several times a week to tell me he had to work late, and that went on for months."

She'd been mad at Chad's boss for taking advantage of Chad's work ethic, had even felt sorry for Chad working so hard. It made what he did feel like even more of a betrayal. But she didn't tell Nick that part because she didn't want him thinking she was gullible.

She did tell him how she'd caught her husband in the act. "At first I didn't believe it when my brother told me my husband was cheating on me, but the next time Chad called to tell me he had to work late, I offered to make his favorite dinner and take it to him. He objected, and when I insisted, he argued. It made me suspicious, so I drove to his workplace. When he left work I followed him, straight to her place. When I peeked through a window later, I saw him on the floor screwing my brother's slutty friend."

"That's it?" he asked, as though he'd been hoping to hear something more salacious.

Feeling an irrational but urgent need to justify her actions, Christie told him, "Looking through his briefcase a few days later I found a receipt from a lawyer who specializes in divorce."

Nick raised an eyebrow and said, "If Chad divorces you, you'll only get half the money, but if he's dead you'll get it all plus his life insurance, is that it?"

Furious at him for suggesting she didn't deserve the money, even after what her husband had done to her, she whispered angrily, "I'm paying you to kill him, end of discussion."

Nick asked her if she'd confronted her husband.

"Are you going to do this, or not?"

"Yeah, sure, but I need an address, don't I?"

Before leaving home she had written the address on a scrap of paper and put it in her coat pocket. As she pushed it across the table toward Nick, Christie said, "She gets off work at eleven but Chad will be there at eight for the Syracuse game. He's never missed a Syracuse game."

Smiling as though pleased with his cleverness, Nick said, "Well he's gonna miss tonight's game."

Watching Nick raise his glass then tip his head back and drain the whiskey reminded her she was sitting in a dive with a felon. Her anger welled up at Chad for having put her there. "Make the bastard suffer."

"Oh, I plan to have some fun with this," he said.

For Christie the thought of Chad begging for mercy as he died a slow agonizing death was immensely satisfying, but then

Nick suggested, "You should come with me," which ruined the moment, because she couldn't stomach the sight of gore.

"You call me when it's done," she said. "That was the deal."

Having already finished his own drink, Nick raised hers, saluting her with it before he drained it. She found his insolence appalling, and the show of disrespect infuriating, but she was at a loss for words.

He stood up, said, "Time to teach someone a lesson," then dropped a crumpled bill on the table before walking away.

Afraid someone might see her with Nick and remember her later, Christie waited several minutes before leaving. Trying to appear casual, she fought the urge to hurry past the two sleazy-looking deadbeats sitting at the bar on her way out. And once outside, she had a long slow walk to her car, which she'd parked in a lot a block away so it wouldn't be visible from the street.

When she was safely behind the wheel of her car she took several deep breaths to regain her composure. Then to kill time until Nick called to say Chad was dead, Christie drove around aimlessly with her cell phone on the passenger seat waiting for it to ring. She checked her phone several times to be sure it was on, that the battery hadn't gone dead, and that she hadn't turned off the ringer by accident.

The next time she heard Nick's voice, she'd be rid of Chad. When the call finally came she nearly had an accident, swerving into the oncoming lane, almost hitting a car. In his irritating, gravelly voice Nick told her he wanted the rest of his money. All Christie had to do was pay the foul little man the other half of his fee then she could celebrate Chad's demise.

Arriving at the girlfriend's place in a daze, with little recollection of the drive, Christie parked on the street half a block away so the neighbors wouldn't remember her car later if the police questioned them. She walked to the door slowly so she'd look like a casual passer-by, prepared to walk past the place if she noticed anyone watching.

She knocked twice.

* * * *

When Nick opened the door Christie rushed in past him and crossed the room, as though she wanted to get as far away from him as possible.

When he demanded the rest of the money she tossed an envelope on the kitchen counter and asked, "Did you make him suffer?"

Christie cowered and backed away as Nick approached her to get the envelope. Amused by the arrogant woman's show of fear, he was tempted to yell "Boo" at her, but he didn't want her to bolt. As he leaned in toward her to retrieve the envelope he was surprised to smell the delicate scent of lilac on her. He wondered what kind of woman would wear perfume to her husband's murder.

Then, after stepping sideways to get between Christie and the door, he took a piece of cloth and a small bottle out of his coat pocket. He poured some liquid onto the cloth then placed the bottle on the counter, and for just a moment, they faced each other silently. Christie looked as though she wanted to ask him something but wasn't sure what. Nick savored the moment.

By the time she decided to run for the door it was too late. She'd barely shifted her weight before he had one hand around her waist and the cloth held over her mouth with the other. She struggled briefly before succumbing to the chloroform.

Nick carried her into one of the bedrooms, enjoying the irony of the expression "dead weight" as he dropped her onto the bed. After he'd tied her up and put tape over her mouth, he sat in a chair next to the bed to wait.

When he heard Christie moan some time later, he slapped her face to bring her around. She blinked a few times, looking bewildered at first. Then the confusion seemed to clear. When she saw the body next to her on the bed she struggled against the ropes binding her hands and feet.

Nick gave her a minute to think about her situation before

he told her, "If you look closely, you'll see your husband's still breathing. I had to chloroform him a couple of times, but as for killing him, I've never killed anybody in my life."

Nick waited for Christie to work through another fit of thrashing before saying, "You gotta ask yourself why I'd risk getting the electric chair when I can take your money without killing anybody."

He took the chloroform and the rag out of his pocket, making sure Christie saw them. "I want you to know," he said, "that I told your husband you hired me to kill him."

Shaking his head in an affected display of sorrow, Nick added, "I'm afraid he didn't see the humor in it. And what do you suppose his girlfriend is going to think when she comes home and finds the two of you lying in her bed naked?"

DEAD LUCKY

few days ago I would have enjoyed standing out on our sixth-floor balcony in the mild autumn weather and warm midday sunshine, but now I'm watching for those fiends to come back.

An old lady in the street below me stumbles among the bodies, as though she's stoned, but she's blinded, another casualty of the virus. I hear a noise and look off in the distance. I know that she heard it too because she turns her head in the direction of the car that's careening towards her.

Ask me how can I stand here and watch what's happening and do nothing to help and I won't have an answer, except to say that I'm scared. I want to yell to the old woman, to warn her that the car isn't going to stop, but I don't because I don't want the brutes in that car to know we're up here. I don't want them to come looking for us.

I hear the car's engine race just before it slams into her, hear the thud as her body absorbs some of the car's momentum. She's airborne for several long surreal moments before she bounces off of a parked car like a rag doll. It sickens me, but I comfort myself with the knowledge that her troubles are probably over, and that nothing I could've done would have made a difference. The first time I saw them kill somebody, I wanted to make them pay for it, but now I'm just glad it's not one of us out there, and I can't remember when I crossed that line.

Four of them are out of the car walking among the bodies.

When they find a live one, they beat it so viciously I can hear the sounds six floors above them. It reminds me of a documentary I saw as a child that showed seal hunters killing baby seals with clubs. The commotion startles a flock of crows feeding on the bodies, the raucous sounds they make as they take flight mingling with the laughter of the car people. I go back inside and close the balcony door to shut it out because it leaves me feeling helpless, frightened, and nauseous.

For all the scary talk about new diseases, and virulent mutations, and drug resistant strains, no one saw this coming, and by the time they realized what was happening, the virus had spread too far. So many people are blind and need help now that there aren't enough of us left with eyesight to care for them. It's death that answers their calls for help.

I go sit on the couch because I need some rest. I hope that the exhaustion I feel is from stress and lack of sleep, not the onset of the virus. I haven't slept much since my wife Mary got the fever because I'm consumed with anger thinking about her lying in the bedroom burning up with a fever that will take away her eyesight, when others, like those murderous bastards outside, are some of the lucky few who might be immune to the virus.

I think about the people who were out of town when it hit. So many people travel these days and so many people tried to flee. I wonder what happens to the ones who wake up blind in unfamiliar surroundings with no one to help them. And all those hospital patients out there; what happens when they call for help and no one comes?

So I think the ones who were at home when the fever hit are the lucky ones, because even if they're blind they can find food. Then I remember the electricity. There won't be any heat with the electricity off. The water pumps must have backup power, but they'll stop soon too, and when the clean water's gone, diseases like cholera and dysentery will sweep through the cities claiming their own victims.

And what about people like me who can still see? We're

doomed to witness the horrors that lie ahead for the ones who are blind, so I think the ones who die are the lucky ones. But that thought leads to madness, because then I think about killing Mary. I contemplate the act, wondering how I would do it, wondering if I could do it. And would it be an act of mercy, or an excuse to rid myself of her because she's a liability? I'm sure I could escape the city on my own, but I'm afraid I won't make it if I bring her with me. I'm angry at myself for thinking of leaving her and I look for something to do to drive these thoughts out of my head.

My eyes have started to itch. It scares me because, before the television went off the air, the experts said that it's an early symptom of the virus. And they said that once the fever takes hold, you slip into a comatose state in a matter of hours that can last for several days. That's what happened to Mary. Now I worry that we could fall prey to the fiends roaming the streets below if I succumb to the virus. I have to get us out of the city before the fever strikes me down, so although Mary is still delirious with the fever, I'm determined to leave today. I'll carry her to the car if I have to. We'll go look for her family upstate.

Now I understand why she tried for years to get me to leave the city. Rural communities are made up of friends and relatives who, regardless of their differences, will come to each other's aid. But in the cities, where our survival can depend on the goodwill of strangers, people have always been wary of them, and it's worse now because any one of them could be a carrier of the virus. The disenfranchised and disillusioned have always been drawn together by poverty and pushed together by population pressures. Now groups of them roam the streets looking for revenge.

I hear Mary stirring. She calls out my name. She's scared; I hear it in her voice, so I hurry to the bedroom and tell her, "I'm here, hon."

As I enter the room she sits up and says, "I can't see, Andy."

Her voice is shaky. I've never seen her look so frail, but even after running a high fever for two days, she's still beautiful.

Her flawless complexion is pale, but the classic lines of her nose and mouth are still as finely sculpted and delicate as they were the day we met. Makeup is smeared around the eyes that once drew me in but now appear lifeless, and sweat from her fever has soaked the sheets causing her soft, black hair to hang in damp clumps against her face.

She puts her arms out to grab me as I get close to her. I lie to her; tell her that it's going to be okay. The lie is easy and makes me feel better, but she continues to shake. She feels small and vulnerable. She squeezes my arm so hard I flinch, as she pleads with me to take her to a hospital. I sit down on the bed next to her and try to put my arm around her, to comfort her, but she pushes me away, urgency and anger in her voice. "I'm not kidding. I need to get to a hospital."

When I ask her if she remembers what was on the news before she got sick, I feel her body become tense. "You're not gonna take me to the hospital, are you?"

I ask her if she remembers the early reports about the virus in Asia.

"Is that what happened to me?"

I don't have the courage to confront her with the truth directly, so I tell her that the CDC said the infection rate is over ninety percent.

"But the blindness, it's just temporary, isn't it?"

To answer the question is to take her eyesight from her and the finality of it distresses me, so, like a coward, I evade her question. "You've had a raging fever for two days."

"Answer me, Andy?"

Feeling wretched, I give in and tell her the truth, that they didn't find a cure.

She yells, "No," then begins to hit me with her fists like an angry child, stopping moments later, as if she has just remembered something. I watch her stand up, grasping at the air until she finds the headboard and latches onto it to steady herself.

She looks in my general direction. "I don't care what you

heard on TV, I have to get to a hospital."

"There are no hospitals."

She snaps at me. "Of course there are hospitals."

The experts had debated over where it came from, and why it was so virulent, and why it attacked the optic nerve, but all of their talk came to nothing. I hear myself telling her that the doctors and nurses were blinded too.

Then her anger flares again. "But, you can see, can't you?"

Feeling guilty and desperate for her forgiveness, I reach over to take her hand and pull her back onto the bed with me, but she draws her hand away, as though burned by my touch.

She tells me to call nine-one-one, and when I hesitate she yells, "Damn it, Andy, call nine-one-one."

"I tried that, and I tried every hospital and every doctor in the phone book. I hear the dial tone and I hear it ring, but no one ever answers."

"What about the cell phone?"

I nod out of habit, then, realizing my mistake, I tell her I tried that too.

"What are they saying on TV?"

"There is no TV. The electricity's off. I think the grid crashed."

"I don't give a shit about the stupid grid, Andy. I need a doctor."

I wish I could think of something to say to ease her distress but I can't. She closes her clouded eyes and breathes slowly, as though she's meditating. After she calms down a little, she asks me what I heard before the power went off.

"The television stations all showed warnings telling people to stay indoors to avoid the virus. They just let them repeat until the power went off."

Mary backs up toward me until her legs hit the edge of the mattress. Then she sits down on the bed, landing hard, as though she's defeated, and I feel like I failed her as a man because I couldn't protect her. Once again I reach for her, and once again she struggles, but not as hard as before.

I hold on tighter this time, and before I realize that I'm opening a door I can't close, I say, "I'm gonna take you someplace safe."

"Safe? What the hell does that mean?"

"There are some very bad people roaming the streets..."

She interrupts me. "Maybe they know where we can find a doctor."

While I wonder how much I should tell her, she asks me how I know they're bad.

"Because I stood on our balcony and watched them killing people in the street below."

She shakes her head slowly. "They wouldn't get away with that."

"Mary, there's no one left to stop them."

As she stands there and shakes her head at me, I try very hard to think of a way to convince her, but I can't, so I decide to take her out on the balcony and let her hear what they do. I warn her to be quiet, tell her that our lives depend on it. Then I lead her out of the bedroom, walking backwards because the hallway is too narrow for us to walk side by side. Mary bumps into the hall table, knocking over a porcelain vase that was valuable just a few days ago. The noise startles her when it hits the floor and shatters. I kick the pieces aside so her bare feet won't step on them.

I remind her to be quiet before I slide the door open and lead her carefully out onto the balcony. Day or night, the sound of traffic has always been a constant for us, but the muffled, indistinct cries of injured and dying people are the background noise in this perverse new version of the city.

I feel Mary's body twitch when an injured man cries out for help. She pleads with me. "Do something, Andy."

It's spooky the way the car people seem to respond to her. They come out of the building across the street, their laughter jarring my nerves as they search through the injured for signs of life. They beat everyone, even the ones that aren't moving and may already be dead; the sounds of bones breaking as crisp and clear as the sound of snapping twigs on a forest path. Even the muffled sound of a baseball bat connecting with flesh carries all the way up to our balcony. I take Mary back inside when she begins to sob, pulling her away from the windows so they can't see us.

Then I scurry about the apartment gathering the things I think we'll need for the trip upstate, while Mary sits on the couch without moving or talking, as though she's slipped into another coma. I pack some medicine and enough food for a couple of days in a small backpack because I'll need my hands free to help her.

My eyes still itch and I'm getting congested and a little lightheaded, so I take cold pills, double the dose, and put the rest of them in my pocket. Thinking maybe I can keep the fever and the blindness at bay by staying awake, I bring a baggie full of coffee grounds to chew on.

When I've packed everything I think we'll need, I guide Mary into the hallway without bothering to close the door because we won't be coming back. This is the only place we've ever lived, but I don't stop for a last look because Mary can't share it with me.

I thank God that we live on the sixth floor and not any higher because, with the electricity out, the elevators aren't working. At first, the light from our apartment spilling into the hallway helps me to see, but once we're in the stairwell, it's as black for me as it is for Mary, blacker than any night I can remember. She doesn't know that it's dark in the stairwell, but I don't feel right complaining to her about it. I hold the railing as I guide her down the stairs, but in the absolute blackness of the stairwell, she could just as easily be helping me, so it takes us a long time to get down the twelve flights of stairs to the lobby.

I see a young boy there, maybe seven or eight years of age, sitting on the floor leaning against the wall. He hears us and looks in our direction, but his eyes don't meet mine because he too is blind. He looks frightened but I have very little strength and compassion beyond what I'll need for Mary, and yet I can't leave him behind for the car people to find. I take Mary over to the boy. He's dirty and smells of urine because he's wet himself. I know he hears me approaching because he tries to crawl away. When I touch his shoulder, he begins to hit me but I manage to get hold of his arms.

He sounds as small and scared as he looks, begging me not to hurt him as he tries to pull free of my grip.

When I assure him that he's safe with us he begins to cry, telling us between sobs that he's hungry, so I take off the backpack to get him something to eat. I put a piece of bread in his hands and, while he eats it, I tell him that I'm going to get our car; that we're going someplace safe and that we'll take him with us.

Then I take one of his hands and put it in my wife's hands. "This is Mary. You stay here with her and be very quiet."

I lie to them; tell them that I'll find someone who can help them when we get upstate. I may be signing our death warrant by taking the boy with us, but how can I leave him behind?

I go to the glass entryway at the front of the building to look outside. Those fiends are still out there and I try not to think about what they'll do to us if they catch us. They're looking the other way, busy with something and I don't want to think of what it might be. Our car is parked on the street between them and me. It would be an easy, short walk any other day but I'm so scared that it might as well be death's own doorway I have to walk through. My legs feel watery and weak. I'm unsure of my feet but I push the door open anyway.

I crouch low and move very carefully along behind the parked cars until I get to our car. I check to be sure that they're not looking then take a deep breath before I walk around the car, unlocking the driver's door with the key so the car won't beep. Then I open the door slowly and get in, slouching in the seat so I'm below the window, pulling the door closed without latching it.

I need a moment to calm my nerves. I take another cold pill and some pain pills, chewing them up and swallowing them dry. Before starting the car I think about getting Mary and the boy from the lobby to the car and I don't see how it's possible. When I start the car, they'll hear it and come for me. Faced with that prospect, it's very hard for me to summon the courage to move and when I do, I sit up just enough to peek out the window.

They're looking around and I'm afraid that I've missed my chance. I'm tempted to drive away. I tell myself that they might follow me; that I could lead them away from Mary and the boy; that I could come back later, but I'm afraid that's not what would happen. I'm afraid I might not come back.

The car starts easily and they hear it. They're looking in my direction. I gun the engine, swerving out into the road, then around a body and onto the sidewalk in front of the lobby. I stop the car with the passenger doors next to the lobby entrance. That'll make it easier to get Mary and the boy in the car. But I'll have to go around the car to get them, and again when I come back, and I'll be out in the open when I do.

Those fiends are close now and they're coming fast. I won't have enough time to get both Mary and the boy in the car, so I decide to leave the boy. I hit the unlock button on the door handle as I get out of the car so I can open the passenger door when I come back with Mary. My legs tremble. I have to will them to move because I'm afraid that time has run out for us.

As I run around the front of the car, I spot a man carrying a tire iron running toward me. He's closing the distance between us quickly, too quickly, so I stop and begin to backup. Then he shudders and lurches forward, as though someone has given him a body block. As a grisly looking mass of viscera erupts from his chest, I hear a pop from somewhere off in the distance. I freeze next to the driver's door and scan the buildings, spotting movement high up on a balcony a block away. I hear the gun again and see another one of the car people drop as his head explodes.

I decide the shooter must have a scope on his rifle to be so accurate at such a distance; probably one of those survivalists. There was a time when I would've called someone like that a nut case, but now I want to yell out, "Kill the bastards," and I would have if he wasn't too far away to hear me.

The last of the car people are crouched down behind parked cars watching the shooter. It's their turn to cower in fear. There's some satisfaction in that.

I force myself to walk around the car the last few feet to the lobby door. One of the car people sees me and we lock eyes for a moment. It gives me a chill, but he doesn't come out of his hiding place. The shooter has bought us some time, and probably saved our lives.

I'm reaching for the lobby door when I'm hit in the back with such force that I'm slammed against the lobby window. At first I'm confused because I didn't think anyone was that close to me. I assume that the man with the tire iron did it, but then I remember his chest exploding. As I slump to the ground, I see blood smear the window and I know that it's mine, and I realize that the man with the rifle thought I was one of the car people.

I can see Mary and the boy through the lobby window, and I worry about what will happen to them.

PLEDGE OF ALLEGIANCE

I was sitting on my bed when I heard the front dooropen. Moments later my six-year-old grandson, Matt, barged into my bedroom holding up a plastic-coated card with Magi-Corp's 3D logo on it and announced, "Mommy said you'd help me learn the Pledge of Allegiance."

I hated Magi-Corp and everything they stood for, but how could I refuse the little guy after seeing the look of anticipation on his face? A lanky little kid with fine red hair and a ruddy complexion, Matt was definitely my progeny.

When my daughter Kaylene appeared in my doorway I told her, "This is a nice surprise," and tried my best to sound sincere.

Although a grimace and a sideways look told me what she was thinking she said it anyway. "I don't want to hear it, Dad."

Afraid that she'd leave and take Matt, and that I wouldn't see him again for a long while, I lied to her. "I mean it, Kaylene. I missed you guys."

My reward for being magnanimous was her saying, "Promise me I won't regret bringing him."

This time would be different. I wouldn't say anything to provoke her. That thought was still in my head when I noticed that Matt, who had always been a skinny pale little kid, looked even worse than usual. "He spends too much time indoors playing with that damn electronic thing."

Matt didn't let my obvious ignorance pass. "It's an Experience Enhancer, Grampa,"

And it earned me another warning from Kaylene. "What'd I just say, Dad?"

So much for behaving. But I couldn't help it. Matt's lack of physical development really worried me. If he was my kid I'd send him outside to play, every day, and I wouldn't let him come back in until the streetlights came on. "He's turning into a powder-puff, Kaylene." I left out the part about her being a parentally challenged mother.

After rolling her eyes and giving me a look of affected exasperation she'd perfected when she was a teenager, she told me, "I'm not going to warn you again, Dad" then left the room.

I felt a gentle tug on my shirtsleeve. "Grandpa?"

The little guy sounded impatient. I guess I'd drifted off. I do that more often these days. He was holding Magi-Corp's card out toward me. After giving it a quick once-over, I asked him about the phone number on it.

"That's so I can call for help."

He took it from me then turned it over and handed it back. That side had the word "Pledge" on it in big red letters. I was glad to have the time with my grandson, but the thought of helping him memorize a piece of corporate propaganda troubled me. "Do you really want to learn this?"

He nodded his head solemnly. "I have to recite it for my class tomorrow. If I get it wrong, they'll send me to the HR officer."

Hearing him say "HR" startled me. "You mean the principal, don't you?"

"No, silly. The human resource officer."

Although it might've just been one of those silly changes in terminology every generation makes, it sent a chill up my spine, not only because Magi-Corp was behind it, but because the term "officer" suggested policeman. I asked him what would happen to him if he got sent to HR.

"It'll go on my record. Whatever that means. But they'll tell Mom about it and she'll get mad. Then she'll tell my dad and he'll get even madder than Mom. And the kids in my class will tell the kids in the other classes. Then none of the kids at school will talk to me, ever."

Kids do exaggerate. Kaylene had been a real drama queen when she was his age. That's probably who Matt got it from. He had crossed his scrawny little arms over his chest and pooched his lower lip out. Rather than upset him further I dropped the HR business. "Well then," I said, holding the card up close to my eyes with a liver-spotted hand so I could read it, "let's get to work."

The pledge, printed beneath Magi-Corp's 3D logo, started with, "I pledge allegiance to Magi-Corp, and to the values for which it stands, one corporation, under God, enhancing the quality of life for all."

That wasn't all of it, but it was enough to set off all kinds of alarms in my head. Children pledging allegiance to a financial institution was pure evil. And the words "under god" implied that their corporate doctrine was somehow righteous. It ended with the word "Amen," suggesting that Magi-Corp required a spiritual commitment from Matt. The implications for his future frightened me.

Matt stood up causing my rickety old bed to sway, the motion startling me. Apparently I'd drifted off again.

Pointing at the paperback book on my lap, he asked, "What's that, Grandpa?"

I held my dilapidated but cherished copy of <u>1984</u> up to show him.

He tipped his head and frowned. "Where'd you get it, Grandpa?"

As I pulled the cardboard box that held my cherished collection of books out from under my bed, I lamented the passing of book stores and libraries.

He looked at them with what I supposed was curiosity

then said, "I saw some of those when our class went to the museum."

I held up <u>The Cat in the Hat</u> and patted the bed next to me. "Come. Sit. I think you'll like this one."

He stepped back, shaking his head vigorously, as though the book would bite him. Eying me warily he said, "My teacher told us those are bad."

"Your teacher tells you what's good and what's bad?"

He nodded his head.

"What about Mom and Dad?"

"Yeah, them too."

I didn't tell him what I was thinking - that his teacher and his parents were accomplices to his indoctrination by Magi-Corp. "When I was your age corporations didn't make the rules?"

His eyes got as big as saucers. "You didn't have rules?"

"Sure we had rules. But we elected the people who made the rules."

"Elected, what's that?"

"It means we picked them."

"Why?"

"To ensure that the rules were good for us. You see, we were citizens...."

He interrupted me, announcing, "I'm a good corporate citizen," with way too much enthusiasm.

I told him we were citizens of countries.

Scrunching up his nose as though he'd just gotten a whiff of something that didn't smell quite right, he asked, "What are countries?"

I told him the world was divided up geographically.

"Geo what?"

I figured I was pushing the limits of Matt's pint-size reservoir of patience. "It means places. The world was divided into places."

"Now you're being silly, Grandpa."

"Why is that silly?"

"You can't cut up the world? It's too big."

"Well, no, of course they didn't really cut it up. People belonged to the place where they were born."

"You belonged to a hospital?"

"Matt, Kaylene said harshly. She was standing at the door very stern-faced.

Matt announced that he had to pee then ran from the room. Little boys have always waited too long to pee. At least that hasn't changed.

It was obvious from Kaylene's red face that she was going to yell at me. "Are you crazy, Dad?"

Clueless about what I'd done to set her off, I shrugged my shoulders.

"You're telling him about the old ways."

"It's a book, Kaylene. Since when do you have a problem with books?"

"And countries, you told him about countries."

I couldn't believe the stuff coming out of her mouth. "What am I supposed to do? Pretend the past never happened."

"It's heresy, Dad."

"It's history, Kaylene. How can history be heresy?"

"It's not part of Magi-Corp's approved world view."

I wondered when Magi-Corp had become the official arbiter of history. "My God, Kaylene, do you hear yourself?"

She told me I'd never see Matt again.

"How can you do that?"

"Then not another word about the past. Do you understand?"

How could I agree to something so absurd? "The world has become a moral and intellectual wasteland because we've forgotten how to think for ourselves."

"Stop it, Dad."

Unable to control my anger any more, I lost it. I brought up her new husband, another one of topics that had poisoned our relationship. "That's something you and your new husband should have taught Matt."

"If it wasn't for Roger's job at Magi-Corp you wouldn't

have a place to live. And if it wasn't for me, you wouldn't have anything to eat."

She was right of course. I couldn't afford my rent. Hell, I could barely afford my groceries, and I had no way to get to the store. So I was grateful for the food Kaylene brought and the meals she made for me. But she and Roger weren't the saints she claimed they were. "So you freeze a few meals for me, so what?"

"How dare you?"

"You wouldn't even do that if it wasn't for that idiotic government program. What's it called? Oh yeah, the Family Assistance Mandate. Too bad for you and Roger it requires you to cover my living expenses and healthcare costs."

Red-faced and glaring at me, her voice high-pitched and cracking, she yelled at me again. "Roger pays all of your bills, you ungrateful old bastard."

"And how nice for the wealthy that they no longer pay taxes to support programs for the poor and elderly, like Medicare, and Welfare, and Food Stamps. And how nice for corporations that they're no longer expected to provide pensions or healthcare."

"If Roger wasn't paying for this dump, you'd be on the street."

If there was one thing I couldn't stomach, it was the thought of Roger being my savior. "Don't make him out to be some kind of saint. It's the law. Besides, you and Roger would rather pay for this place than have me move in with you. And isn't it convenient for you that there's no public transportation to your house, and that I don't drive and can't afford a cab, so I can never bother you at home. Hell, Kaylene, in the six plus years you've been married to Roger, I haven't once been to your house."

She had set her jaw. It meant she was having trouble controlling her anger. I remembered her doing that as a kid. "If word gets out that you have a book, or that you were telling Matt about the old days, it'll be a blot on our name we can never erase."

"Oh spare me the theatrics, Kaylene."

"You could get Matt expelled from school and blacklisted.

It would rob him of his future. Is that what you want, Dad?"

I shook my head because I didn't want to lose Matt forever. But he needed protection from the new world, a world where 'up' wasn't up, and 'down' wasn't down any more. But I didn't know what to do about it.

In the meantime, I wasn't going to live in a hovel that my daughter and her husband were paying for against their will. So I took my suitcase out of my closet and opened it on the bed then rummaged through my dresser. Deciding what to take and what to leave behind isn't so easy if you only have one small suitcase and you're so old and frail you can barely carry that.

Kaylene surprised the hell out of me – she came over and put her hand on my arm and squeezed it gently. "Don't do something we'll both regret, Dad."

Matt rejoined us just before Kaylene pulled me into an embrace so unexpected it gave me pause. For a few precious moments, I forgot the years of emotional scars.

Then she gently pushed me away. I stood back and watched her take my clothes out of the suitcase and put them back in my dresser. She said, "We'll figure it out, Dad," as she put my suitcase back in the closet.

I knew better. It didn't matter how many times we swore we'd treat each other with kindness and respect, we always ended up yelling. Our scrapheap of old arguments was piled so high with festering emotional scars that even minor slights and unkind words felt like vicious, deep wounds. "We'll just argue again, Kaylene. You know we will."

"If you won't do it for me, Dad, then do it for Matt."

Even if Kaylene forgave me, her husband would still resent paying my expenses. And I knew they both dreaded the day when I'd need full time care and have to move in with them.

I had pushed her aside and was taking my suitcase back out of the closet when I heard hard-soled boots on the wood floor in the hallway coming toward the bedroom. I looked at my daughter. She looked back at me stonily.

I let her have it. "You called them didn't you, Kaylene?

That's why you hugged me – so I wouldn't leave before they got here."

"All you had to do was keep your subversive bullshit to yourself, but you couldn't do it."

"I'm not like you. I won't lie to the boy."

"You put Matt's future at risk."

"I can't just stand by and let Magi-Corp ruin the future."

"And what do you think one doddering old man can do?"

"Show Matt that I'm willing to face one of Magi-Corp's goon squads for him."

"And what good's that gonna do?"

"Someday he'll wonder why I risked dying rather than surrender to Magi-Corp."

Kaylene was saying, "He won't give it a thought," when three men in SWAT gear burst into the room, their glowing 3D Magi-Corp logos hovering in the air next to their shoulder patches like tiny alien life forms. And Matt had come in with them.

One of the Magi-Corp goons knelt down in front of him and pointed a finger gloved in thick black plastic at me. "Is this the man you called us about?"

"Yes, sir," he said, sounding much too proud, and stretching himself up into a little boy's idea of what standing at attention would look like.

"You did the right thing, son. I'll make sure it's noted on your record."

Beaming a smile almost too big for his face, Matt was clutching his Magi-Corp pledge card in his little hand. I didn't blame him for calling the number on the back of it. How could I? People in my generation were warned about the evil and did nothing. For years Kaylene's generation profited from Magi-Corp's malfeasance. But the day came when Magi-Corp no longer needed their support and turned on them. By then Magi-Corp was too big and they were too afraid to oppose it. So I couldn't very well expect Matt to put the evil genie back in the bottle.

I wanted to yell something at Kaylene, something to ease

my anger and frustration, but I didn't find the words before I was dragged through my front door. As I rode to who knew where in the police van, I wondered what kind of punishment awaited me; no doubt something exceptionally unpleasant then death. At least Matt knew how to survive. There was some solace in that.

The End

www.ingramcontent.com/pod-product-compliance
Lightning Source LLC
Chambersburg PA
CBHW071522170626
46811CB00007B/2927